Over the Dunes *a Rider* Comes

Vaughn Hansen

Over the Dunes Press—Lamar, IN
ISBN: 979-8-3304-1015-6
Title: *Over the Dunes a Rider Comes*
Author: Vaughn Hansen
Digital distribution | 2024
Paperback | 2024

Second Edition

DEDICATION

This book is dedicated with love to my mother and Stepfather Lois and Ralph Whitaker.

With thanks to my sister Amy and friends Kaydell Leavitt, Jason Clem, and Adam Loahr, and my publisher Erica Hughes who without their support and encouragement this book would not have been possible.

CHAPTER 1

A hot wind blew across the desert stirring up small swirls of sand that danced across the dunes that stretched for miles in all directions. Not even a blade of grass peaked through the lifeless sand. A lone dust devil made its way into a valley formed by the dunes reaching the center of the valley like a spinning top the sands slowly stopped their dance and settled to the ground beneath them.

For a second everything was still once more. A small movement stirred as the first trickle of water started to seep onto the dry sands and quickly began to spread in all directions 'til a cold lake of water stood in the center of the valley. The desert gave way reluctantly, as at the edges of the pool grass and trees shoved their way upward reaching to the sun. Within minutes, the lifeless valley turned into a rich oasis. A pool of cold water bubbling as the air trapped beneath the sand fought its way to freedom. The light shining through the leaves shined on a jewel, sitting on a large flat stone in the center of the water waiting. In the distance, a horse and a rider wearily trudged through the sands.

Over the dunes, a rider comes

The Ronan war had lasted 24 years. The war was fought by two very powerful and wealthy kingdoms over the mining rights to a mountain range on a shared border. The final battle involved seventy-five thousand soldiers from both sides, and had lasted a full fortnight, and ended in a stalemate. Both kingdoms worn and battle weary, had called for a truce. The irony was that the mineral rich mines that both kingdoms had fought and lost so much for had long since been stripped by thieves.

The kingdoms had both turned to trying to rebuild, what was left, of their once great lands. The men who had lived through the war went on their separate ways onto the next battle or war.

This was not the first time that Ashes had seen such a thing and he was sure that it would not be the last. If there was one thing that man seemed to be good at it was killing each other. He was forty-two years old as best as he could recall, old for a mercenary. All that he had to show for his forty-two years of life was his saddle, his saddlebags, his sword, knife, a few coins, and his horse. In his line of work a man's life depended on a good horse -- just as much as a good sword. If you could not fight your way out of a battle, then you had better have a horse that could outrun the other army.

The horse that he rode now, was the fourth that he had owned. The other three had all been good animals. To this day he mourned their loss. Two had died in battle and one had fallen ill and died. The stallion that he rode now he had given the name "China" it had been his only sister's name she had died young of illness. Like her, the stallion had a strong stubborn streak which reminded him of her. They had been together for eight years and China had carried him through many dangers. None of those dangers were as great as the one that they faced now.

The desert that they were crossing was dangerous but not impassable. He had crossed it twice before in his lifetime. Both times he had sworn that he would never cross it again. The heat was bad but the real danger was that the winds never seemed to stop changing the landscape making it impossible to rely on landmarks. To add to their troubles, they had run into a trio of thieves two days ago. The thieves had thought that they had found easy prey. And had paid for their mistake. Ashes had won the battle, but he lost his water. A sword stroke from one of the thieves slit his water bag and, as luck would have it the thieves' water bottles were empty.

This was the second day that they went without water. Ashes knew that he could last, maybe two more days, but China would not last that long and was growing weak. The sand seemed to pull at his hooves, making him stumble.

Ashes slid out of the saddle; he patted the horse's neck, "Come on you can't tell me that the same horse that charged through the Ronan Elite Guard is going to let a little heat beat him. Just think, three days, at most, and we will be in Targa, where you will have the best food, the best grain, all the water you can drink and some of the prettiest mares in any kingdom; all just waiting for a stallion like you."

As Ashes led the way, up the dune, a shadow passed. Putting his hand to his eyes he could see the shapes of the vultures circling them. "Bastards!" he muttered, "go find someone else to stalk -- you won't..." his words were cut off by a sudden jerk on the reins as China threw his head up his nostrils flaring wide in a deep breath. "What is it, boy?! You smell something?"

In answer, the horse started to pick up his pace passing his rider, as he trotted over the rise. Water! It had to be! Staggering he followed the horse's hoof prints in the sand.

Ashes drew his sword as he went, "Blasted horse!" there may be water on the other side but that did not mean that there was also not any danger. Ashes topped the dune ready for anything, but what he found.

CHAPTER 2
The Jewel

The oasis was not a big one but no less amazing. The palms were thick and healthy as was the grass growing around them but the most amazing thing was the pool that gave them life. Even from where Ashes was standing he could see that the pool was clear and cold if not very deep. It seemingly defied the desert on all sides of it.

After looking, to make sure that they were alone Ashes dropped to his belly to drink. The water seemed to both burn and soothe his throat on the way down. Rising, he started to strip off China's saddle and bridle letting the horse wander to graze before picking some fruit off a nearby tree. As he reached for the fruit something flashed in the corner of his eye, His hand dropped to his sword but stopped mid reach when he saw what had caught his attention. In the center of the pool, something flashed again. In the fading sunlight it was not the water itself. Something else seemed to be floating on the surface. Curious he waded out, testing each step for drop offs and hidden trip ups making his way to the center of the pool he saw just above the water line, a curved rock serving as a pedestal for a jewel the size of a man's hand.

The sun's last rays lit up the jewel like a small fire throwing dancing light both on him and on the water filling him with wonder. If only for a second, a second that passed quickly. Another thought went through his mind. "Trap!" Spinning around, in the water, he took in everything, the darkening oasis his grazing horse the trees but there was nothing else. They were alone. Reaching for the jewel for the first time he saw the words carved in the stone that held the jewel. "All that a man could want, all that a man could have. All that a man could dream off. For these you need only wish."

"Wishes?!" he muttered bitterly, "You cannot eat or drink wishes. They will buy you nothing at any market place-- nothing that I know of! Let the women and children keep the wishes. I would rather have my sword and horse any day. I know I can count on them!"

Turning in the water, he started back to the edge of the pool stopping, he looked back at the words one last time; a foolish thought crossed his mind. What if this was real? What would he want? "I have had money, women, and good friends. All of that was taken from me by the same thing, the same thing that has also kept coins in my pocket; the money and women were fleeting. I knew that they would be short-lived, but my friends, them I would give up every coin I ever had to ride beside again but they have gone onto their—I hope, peaceful rewards. It would be wrong to bring them back to the hate and greed of this world and I am not ready yet to join them so if you want to give wishes..." He took a minute to ponder, "Peace," he said softly, "I wish for peace, this world has seen too much of wars, suffering and death. Give this world a good man who could bring peace to these lands, and keep the people safe."

Laughing bitterly, he turned back to the shore. "That's my wish though I doubt very much that I will live long enough to see my wish come true." Wading to the shore he left a trail of water drops on the ground as he walked past his horse. The stallion poked his muzzle at the jewel, sniffing at it questioningly. Ashes used his empty hand to gently push the inquiring muzzle aside. "Uh uh, this is not for your belly. Seeing as how I won't be getting any wishes out of it, I mean to at least get enough coin to keep us both fed for a moon or two."

He ignored the horses irritated tail swish as he picked up the saddle bags.

Putting the jewel in the bags he sat them on the ground then he pulled off his boots to dry. His clothes were still wet from the pool. He stripped down and hung his clothes on a tree trunk to dry as he slept. It was not a cold night so he would sleep warm enough without them. He kept his sword at his side. As he stretched out on the grass using the saddle bags as a head rest he watched the horse graze before he drifted off to sleep trusting the stallion to warn him, if there was any danger....

The stallion wandered the oasis grazing as the night darkened and the moon climbed to its zenith. Then went to stand beside the man who he trusted with his life. Knowing they were in a strange place he raised his head and inhaled deeply checking for any threats before resting a hind leg and nodding off to sleep. They were both light sleepers, but neither he nor Ashes sensed the soft pulsing light that came from the saddle bags as they slept....

CHAPTER 3
Rude Awaking

"Good morning my Lord," Ashes was moving, before his eyes were fully open; his hand grabbing for his sword as he rolled to his feet only to come up with a handful of linen. Confused he looked around taking in everything the oasis the trees, the pool, and most importantly, his horse were all nowhere to be seen. Ashes stood naked next to a bed of fine linen in a room in which the likes of he had only heard of in stories. Marble floors and pillars gave way to stained glass windows that threw the sunlight into the room like a thousand diamonds. The bed and dresser might as well have been cut from pure gold; the wood was so well oiled and polished. A great patio with its doors open stood at the other end of the room. In the middle of all this stood three very concerned-looking men, watching him uncertainly.

Ashes barely heard as the man in the middle spoke again, "Is everything alright Sire? We did not mean to startle you but you did say you wanted to see us at first light." The man who spoke was light haired and had a full beard. He stood seven inches over six feet, and like the other two men he was covered in chain mail from his shoulders to his waist. He carried a heavy sword and two daggers at his side. Also, like his companions he looked very capable of using them.

The other two men could not have looked more like father and son if they tried; one being only slightly smaller than the other but much less grey haired. Ashes tried desperately to recall anything that would tell him how he had come to be here when the memories came flooding to him. Memories that were both strange and familiar at the same time. One memory that stood out—far more real than the others— the *jewel*. His eyes quickly went around the room to the chair in the corner, and his saddle bags. Walking over to the chair, he paid no attention to the worried looks the men gave each other he picked up the saddlebags and opened the flap. The jewel still rested in the bottom throwing off a soft blue light, even though no light reached it.

"This has to be a dream!" Ashes thought, "None of this is real!" Just then, a hand came down on his shoulder, Ashes looked around at the older of the dark haired men, his name coming to him like the other memories

Diego, a lifelong friend, "Rough night? You look like a man who just found out his lady for the night last night was his long lost sister." The smile and friendly eyes relaxed Ashes. He closed the saddle bags and sat it back on the chair.

"You know that your king could have you beheaded for speaking to him like that? Not that that would make you any less annoying, or smell any worse." Turning, Ashes found his clothes sitting on a chair along with his sword.

As Ashes started to dress the man who first spoke stepped toward the patio Fredrex also a long time friend and commander of Ashes' armies. The name came to Ashes like the other memories.

"The troops have gathered as you ordered Sire. We will be ready to march, within the hour, to the Northern borders. The scouts have confirmed that the Obamnas have joined up with the armies from Hllibs, Odeans and Reaidess. They are three days march from our borders. We should have no trouble stopping them there."

Pulling on his boots he walked over to the open patio doors and looked out. The sound of trumpets and the rattle of armor both on men and horses reached him. Looking down into the courtyard even he was impressed. The rows of soldiers filled the big courtyard and stretched out of the gates to the fields beyond. The men looked well-fed and healthy as did the horses. The soldiers and horses moved with a purpose that he had seldom seen in a fighting force.

Nottie, Diego's son and the youngest of the three men spoke for the first time "We gave them your message sire but they did not want to hear it. Libbor has not forgiven you for his son's death. He still thinks that we withheld the medicine that would have saved the boy's life, He will not accept that we did not have a cure; that there is no known cure for the wood curse."

The wood curse was a sickness that was carried by the biting flies in the deep woods of the Norgin Pass. It was rare, seeing as how very few men ever traveled that far into the woods and ever came out. Ashes was sure that it was because of the illness and danger in those woods -- not the spooks and demons, said to be living there.

"Libbor has always been walking on the edge of madness. His son's death has pushed him over that edge," Ashes spoke over his shoulder as he watched the men drilling below. "I pity him for that, and mourn the loss of his son, but there is nothing I could do then for his son just as there is nothing I can do now, for him. I have no wish to go to battle against him or his allies nor will I run from them."

Turning back to the room he walked to the far wall. Where a fine mural was painted, a map, showing the kingdom and all the surrounding lands.

Using his finger, he followed the outline of the kingdom on the map. Stopping at the Northern border and the mountain range that stood between the two lands.

"The only way for Libbor to bring his troops is over Thunder Gorge, and there is only one bridge crossing the gorge. Even if we left now, it is still a four-day march. We would not get there before Libbor would, but if we sent a party of twenty men on fast horses they might get there in time to burn the bridge."

"Burn the bridge?" the shocked voice was Nottie's.

"Sire, that bridge has spanned the gorge for more than six generations. It is the only way over Thunder Gorge and to the Northern Sea. It would take many months to rebuild!"

"Yes, that is true, pup," Diego said with a slight edge to his voice. "But as your king was saying, it is also the only way for Libbor to cross into our lands. If we can stop them from crossing the gorge it might be enough to make Libbor come to his senses, or at least the other leaders, and stop the loss of a great many lives. Only a foolish leader wastes the lives of his men.

Ashes turned to face the three men speaking again. "The riders may not get there in time, so we need to prepare for if they do cross. Send riders to all the outlying villages and farms, and tell them to get all the people to the city. That will take time, so send the riders now!"

Turning back to the map he pointed again with his finger. This time he pointed to a mountain range at the Southern end of the kingdom. "The farmers have already moved the herds to the winter graze in the Hot Springs Valley. Have they not?" As Fedrex nodded assent, Ashes went on. "Good, they will be safe there. The valley is hard to find but still, I want one hundred men there just in case. Send the pack with them as well I know there are only a handful of the pack left, but very few outside of the city know that. Seeing even a few of them might be enough to make anyone think twice about attacking the valley."

Fredrex laughed softly, "I will tell her, but Abby is not going to like that."

"No, she is not," Ashes agreed. "Tell her that I gave the order. If she wants to argue about it, she can find me."

"Also tell the men bringing the villagers, to burn the crops, after the people are safely away."

This time all three men looked shocked. "Burn the crops sire?! Winter is only two months away. There are a great many people who need those crops to get through the winter."

Ashes turned once more to face his friends, "There is more than enough food in the city store to feed the people through the winter, and there is enough seed, as well, to replant in the spring. If Libbor and his troops make it over the pass and are determined to start a war it very well may be that we do stop them at the border -- and this is all for naught, but I will not take the chance that they get by us. I do not want to be feeding them as well as fighting them. The livestock will be safe and well guarded. We can re-grow the crops and replenish the stores when the war is over." Walking past the men, he repeated himself, "Give the order to burn the crops."

CHAPTER 4
A Promise

As Ashes left the room he headed down the hallway and went down the stairs searching through the castle for the one person in his new memories that he almost hoped he would not find. Stopping a passing guard he asked, "Have you seen Summer?"

The guard dipped his head in respect "The queen my lord? Yes, I saw her just a moment ago in the stable."

Ashes thanked the guard and made his way to the stables. The stables were in a building kitty-corner to the castle. Large and well made; warm in the winter and with large enough doors to make them breezy and cool in the Summer; smaller doors on both sides leading to the paddocks and the pastures beyond. It was in the farthest stall that he found who he was looking for.

Summer, his queen, the only women that he ever loved. Before he found the jewel he had left her standing both angry and crying. Back then he had nothing to offer her but a hard life and the chance of being a young widow. He loved her too much to put her through that so he had left her. That was many years ago. He never thought that he would see her again, yet here she stood. He hesitated. Would she know of their past in this place?! Summer was brushing her horse a white appaloosa with faint brown spots.

Summer spoke to the horse as she brushed him. "You're getting fat Dugly we need to go for more rides to work off that grain. You have been getting..." Tossing his head the stallion snorted over his shoulder at her. Earning him a soft slap in return. "Mind your manners stud. Remember who is mistress here, or you will find yourself somewhat lighter in the back end than you would like. I do not need two bullheaded males in my life. Neither of you are as clever as you think when it comes to trying to get by me with something." Summer spoke the last statement over her shoulder. "Are you going to say something to me or are you just going to stand there like a lout? "That is the reason that you're here is it not? To tell me you're leaving?"

"So it is a lout that I am now?" stepping closer Ashes rested his hand on the stall wall just above her shoulder trapping her between him and the stall wall. "Is that how a queen addresses her king?"

"When her king is acting like an ass! Yes!" Summer spoke as she pushed Ashes back enough to get by him. "Who do you think you are -- not telling me about Libbor amassing armies against us?! I should not have to hear about such a thing from the captain of the guard!" When were you going to tell me?! Before or after the battle?! I am your queen as well as your wife, Damn you! And don't tell me you were trying to protect me!"

Taken aback, Ashes gently laid the back of his hand on the side of her face. "I never said anything to you about it because I was unsure about how true the rumors were, I wanted to wait 'til the scouts returned with their reports before saying anything. I was wrong. I am sorry. You are the last person I would hurt."
Summer met his gaze, the anger leaving her eyes. "And are the reports true? Does Libbor intend to wage a war against us?"

"Yes," Ashes spoke softly. "He has gotten the Hillibs the Odeans and the Reidess to join him. They are marching on Thunder Gorge now. I have sent riders to burn the bridge over the gorge before they get there but the riders may not get there in time so I will be taking our troops to meet them at the border just in case."

Summer dropped her gaze as he went on, "I have given orders for the farmers and villagers to be brought back to the city. They will be safer here. The livestock are at the winter graze so they should be safe, if all goes well Libbor will come to his senses and there will be no war."

Summer stepped away from him and began brushing on her stallion once more, "But you don't think that's going to happen. Do you?"

"No," Ashes walked past her to his own horse, as he spoke "A man who gathers such a big army means to use it if we cannot stop them at the gorge there will be a war."

Ashes started brushing China getting the stallion ready for his saddle. He liked doing such things himself. As he was putting the saddle on the stallion, a hand touched his shoulder.

Summer's voice was soft but determined. "I want to come with you. You know I can fight as well as any man. I can take care of myself -- and you know it!"

Ashes chuckled softly" I know very well how you fight and I have had my share of bruises to prove it, but I need you to stay here..." Putting up his hand, to stop her protest, he went on. "You need to be here to protect the people, they will be concerned. You need to be here, to ease their worries." He finished saddling his horse and put his foot into a stirrup and mounted his stallion.

Summer stepped in front of the horse, she stroked the stallion's muzzle as she spoke. "Take care of this oaf," she said softly, "believe it or not I love him as much as you do. He may not do much more than eat and sleep but he has his good points. Please bring him back safely"

A little surprised by her words Ashes assured Summer, "China and I have ridden in many battles together. I have no intent to lose him in this one. I promise that I will bring him back safely!"

Laughing, Summer stepped back, letting the horse move forward. "I was talking to the horse," she said.

CHAPTER 5
A Tough Decision

Ashes guided China out the barn door and headed toward the city gates. Trying hard not to remember the last time he rode away from this women in another place, never to see her again "Not this time!" he thought. "I will be back Summer, I promise!"

Ashes' thoughts were shattered by an angry voice behind him. "Ashes!" Even without turning around he knew its owner. At the sound of hoof beats gaining on him, he reined in China and waited. The other rider caught up with him and turned her mount sideways in front of China, blocking his path. The animal that the women rode was smaller than China with far bigger ears, shorter legs and neck, and a stockier build. Ashes used to wonder why she did not ride a horse instead of her strange mount 'til the battle, on the edge of the Black Tooth Cliffs. Not only was the smaller animal faster than a horse, on the uneven ground, he found footing where there was none. Ashes looked past the donkey's large ears into the angry eyes of his rider. Abby, the captain of the city guard.

"Who do you think you are?" Abby snapped angrily at him.

Ashes had to try hard not to smile despite the anger in the woman's eyes. "What are these two doing?" he wondered. "Working as a team?" Ashes had often wondered if the two were not secretly sisters separated at birth. They could not have been more alike if they tried; he sat back in his saddle waiting as Abby went on.

"Fredrex told me you ordered that the pack go to the hot springs to guard the herds! What gives you the right?! You placed the pack under my protection! Or is that crown sitting so tight on your head that it cut off the blood to your brain and made you forget about that?!"

Sighing, Ashes guided China around the donkey.

"Greetings Brian I see that your rider is as direct as ever." Ashes could not help but smile as the donkey lifted his head and let out an ear splitting bray as if to agree.

"Ride with me, Abby. We need to talk," Abby fell in beside Ashes keeping Brian's head even with China's shoulder showing that much respect for her king despite her angry words. "I know what I said Abby, and nothing has changed. The pack is still yours to watch over."

"How am I supposed to watch over them when you send them away?" Abby asked, still smoldering but subdued "I can't leave the city if you are going off to battle."

Ashes thought carefully as he spoke, he knew how much the pack meant to her and he had a great deal of respect for the woman. She had worked hard to get where she was, proving her bravery and loyalty to him and to the city time-and-time-again. "Abby, there is only, what, nine of the pack left? Out of over one hundred? If the pack is to survive, we have to keep them safe, and the hot springs are the safest place for them. Libbor's riders could look the rest of their lives and never find the Hot Spring Valley. If we go to war, then there might be a chance the war could end up being fought here." He held up a hand stopping her protest.

"No, I don't think that the war will come here, but if it did, can you be sure that the pack would stay safe? They're Warhounds, Abby; it is what they were bred for. It is in their blood. If the fighting did get into the city, the pack would be in the middle of it -- you know they would."

"And, I would be there beside them." Abby said fire burning in her eyes.

"Well, I know that you would give your life for them as they would for you, but think, Abby. In a battle, you cannot keep track of all of them and as strong and fast as they are, they are still just flesh and blood. An arrow or spear could pierce their hearts just as easy as ours. Too many of them have already died fighting our battles, would you lose these last few as well?"

The silence that followed was enough to tell Ashes that his words had had their intended effect. After a few moments Abby said softly. "There are not nine anymore." She smiled slightly as she went, "Angel whelped; three days ago four males and five females all healthy. Bango has not left her side since the birth. I meant to tell you, but never got the chance."

"That is the best news I have heard all day!" Ashes said sincerely. "It has been over ten years since any of the pack has had any young." Warhounds were blessed with a long life span, for their kind, they could live well over thirty years, but with a price. It was rare when they gave birth they had the same cycles and mated as often as others of their kind but rarely conceived.

"The pups' eyes are not even open yet. Neither Angel nor the pups could make such a journey on their own," Abby said worriedly.

"The men that are going to guard the livestock will be taking supplies. Angel and her pups could travel in one of the wagons. It would make the journey easier for her she would not be trying to keep up with the rest of the pack and the pups would be sleeping most of the way."

Ashes made the suggestion carefully. He knew Abby well. She was as headstrong as she was brave. If she got it in her mind that this was going to be bad for the bitch and her pups, then she would fight him tooth and claw over this. And he would have to end up ordering her to do this against her will. He did not want that. He thought too much of her to hurt her that way, and she was one of his most trusted friends and officers. He did not want any bitter feelings between them.

"That's true," Abby answered, "but there are still so many things that could happen on the journey. The pups are very young. If one of the pups fell ill without anyone there who Angel trusted, she wouldn't let anybody near them and the pup could die."

"Angle is not stupid, and she knows and trusts the men in the city guard, what if you sent one of the guards along? Then, if something did happen there would be someone there," Ashes suggested.

"That would be OK, I guess, but still I..." Abby hesitated, trying hard to put her feelings into words without sounding soft.

"You would miss them and worry about them," Ashes finished for her. "You love them, Abby. There is no weakness in saying that. I understand."

"Then why are you making me send them away?!" Abby yelled, startling Brian.

"You know why," Ashes said. "You know I am right; that this would be the best thing for them, but I will not order you to send them away Abby -- not if you don't want to -- I won't do that. I will do worse." Ashes nudged China into a trot, as he spoke, "I am going to let you decide. I know that you love them too much not to do the right thing."

Abby reined in Brian glaring at Ashes back as China trotted away.

"Damn you Ashes! You bastard! You know I hate it when you're right."

The troops were already riding out of the gate when Ashes got to the courtyard. Riding four abreast the column stretched far past the gate. Ashes urged China faster as he rode to the head of the column. Fredrex, Nottie and Diego rode side-by-side, in the lead. Ashes fell in beside them.

"Told you we were missing someone," Nottie said, smiling over at the others.

Diego grunted, "I thought Abby would be spitting out what was left of you by now, or did you just decide that fighting a war would be easier than trying to talk sense into that wildcat and just make a run for it?"

Ashes waited for the laughter to die down from the three and the man within hearing range. He had lived too long to let such things bother him. When it finally did, he gave his friends a long look. "You know, I often think about being a king, what it means caring for the people, making laws, watching the kingdom prosper and grow and basking in the admiration, love and respect of my people, then I come to reality and wonder if it would be wrong to behead my closest friends."

The wind tugged at Summer's blouse, as she stood on the city walls, watching the column disappear in the distance. She wrapped her arms around herself to try to stay warm. It was only early fall but the winds already carried a cold chill.

"I am sure that they will be alright." Surprised, Summer looked over her shoulder at the small women who had spoken. A very pretty woman with a body that could turn many men's heads. Her snow white hair was tied in a ponytail that fell to the middle of her back. Her green eyes seemed to give off a light of their own.

She was a head shorter than Summer who was not a tall woman, herself. Hunters had found her deep in the woods twenty years ago a small bundle lying under a rocky overhang next to a still burning fire. She had been only a few months old then and though the hunters had looked the rest of that day and into the next her mother was nowhere to be found. And there was no clue what had happened to her. Not knowing the baby's name and needing to call her something the hunters gave the baby the name, "Snowflake," because of the child's snow white hair.

Knowing that they would not be able to look after the child the hunters brought her to the city and left her in their care.

Rumors spread about the girl. There had always been tales of elven folk in those woods. Though none of them had ever been seen. Many people in the city believed that this small woman was at least in part, of elven blood.

"Oh, hello Snowflake, you're looking well, how are your gardens doing?" Abby asked.

"Well better this year than last." Snowflake answered her, stepping forward to hug the bigger woman. "Who would believe that one baby goat could do so much damage to a garden in one night!"

"I remember," Summer laughed, "Poor little guy had an upset belly the next day."

Snowflake stepped back from her friend turning her gaze to the city walls and the column of men; now just a faint line in the distance. "Have faith in them, Summer. They will be fine. There are no more loyal or well-trained soldiers in all the kingdoms; and Ashes is no fool."

Reaching down, Snowflake grabbed Summer's wrist and pulled her toward the door. "Now come on, you promised me yesterday that you would go with me looking for fire herb seeds in the woods. I'm not going to let you back out of it"

Abby handed the last pup up to the driver of the wagon and watched as the driver placed the pup in the blankets by its watchful mother.

"There you go Angel," the driver said, "The last of your pups; safe and sound." The pup waddled on stumpy legs over to its mother pushing between its siblings sniffing for a teat to nurse on.

"Just make sure that they stay safe!" Abby snapped, "Or you will have more than a mad mother to deal with."

"Don't worry. I will keep them safe."

"I won't forget about your promise."

The driver answered her as he was taking his place in the seat of the wagon, "I am very fond of my skin and other body parts you threatened to remove if they got hurt"

Abby barely seemed to hear him as she reached down to run a hand across the head of the big dog standing next to her, Chief, the pack leader.

Chief, like all war hounds, was a very big dog; his back reached the belly of the big draft horse standing next to him

He was a big-chested heavily muscled dog with large paws. His black muzzle and saddle markings blended with his silver fur.

Next to Chief, was Bango, Angel's mate, slightly smaller than Chief with brindle markings and a shorter upturned muzzle.

Next to Bango, stood the pack bitch's, Tigress, like Bango, was brindle but with a longer muzzle, and Candy a fawn. Next to her stood Rain the oldest of the pack also a fawn, her muzzle graying with age.

The other two pack males: Worf, and Felix stood close by. One light, one dark, but both brindle.

The last pack member raced across the open field towards the wagon. Brownie was just as tall as her pack-mates but was deep-chested and long-legged with a streamlined head. Her paws thudded on the ground as she raced up skidding to a stop just short of Chief. Chief aimed a warning snap in Brownie's direction, and Brownie backed away.

"That one is the one that concerns me," the wagon's driver said uneasily. "Her eyes. She has the look of someone who has seen the other side of madness."

"I am the one you need to be concerned about!" Abby said as she stepped away from the wagon. "Make sure you take care of all of them, or I will show you the other side of madness! Get on now!"

The last remark aimed at the big horse pulling the wagon slapping his flank

Abby watched as the pack trotted after the wagon, she knew Ashes was right. They would be safer at the hot spring valley, but that did little to ease the ache in her heart that she was already starting to feel.

CHAPTER 6
The Journey

Ashes looked over his shoulder past the long column of men trailing behind him. The city rested against the mountains, walled in on three sides by towering cliffs with huge marble veins running through them. From the cliffs, over thirty generations ago the city had been built. It was at the base of those cliffs that the city's founders had fought a great battle with the Mullbuds, a savage group of raiders who preyed on anyone who they came upon.

After they had driven away the raiders the people laid claim to the land as their home and chose their leaders. Bucken, their first king and his wife, Vanity both had proven their bravery in the great battle and they were very much respected.

The site was chosen and the kingdom was born. It would be twenty years before the city with its great walls was finished. And the city had grown greatly since that time. The city was given the name: "Zlarora" which translated from the old tongue meant: "Star of the plains." It was said that on a bright night, the city's marbled walls and buildings could be seen from over twenty miles away.

The slight uncertainly hung in his mind. He had wished for peace. It seemed so wrong to be riding off to war.

"Would you just sit in your castle and let your people be slaughtered by Libbor and his men?"

The words seemed to come from nowhere, so quiet that he was not even sure that he had heard them. "Your people look to you to lead and protect them. Peace sometimes comes with a heavy price. Only a foolish man wants war. A wise man knows that sometimes it must be."

The army made good time. After two days, Ashes began to think that maybe, they would get to Thunder Gorge before Libbor's army. When messengers arrived from the riders that Ashes had sent ahead to burn the bridge. Three men rode up to the column on sweaty horses. Ashes could tell, even before they spoke, that they did not carry good news. The cuts and dents, on both the men's and on the horse's armor, showed that they had been in a hard fought battle.

The lead rider Thunk, a worn vet of many battles, reined in his horse.

"My king, Libbor's armies have crossed the gorge and have already crossed our borders and attacked the north village.

There are a great many more than we thought sire. I would guess at least twelve thousand. We tried to save as many of the people as we could, but we were badly out- numbered. We got only a small group safely away and hid them in the hills. We left ten men to escort them to the city when it is safe enough to try."

Diego let out a soft curse under his breath.

"They must have ridden their mounts almost to exhaustion to do such a thing. A worn horse is no good in battle -- what are they thinking?"

"They are planning on catching us off guard," Nottie said thoughtfully, "They are counting on us not being ready."

"They know different now," Thunk said bitterly, "We left at least thirty dead and even though they had us beat in numbers their fighting skills and training is very poor. I saw more than one of their men fall to a companion's sword stroke."

"And the rest of your men?" Ashes asked, already knowing the answer.

"Dead, my king, as I said, ten went with the survivors of the village to guard them. The rest of us lead the attackers away. It was a running battle. We did not have time to recover the bodies. I'm sorry."

"You have nothing to be sorry for," Ashes said. "Tell Nottie how to find the villagers, then I want the three of you to go to the healer's wagon and get your wounds and your horse's wounds treated. Eat if you can. Then, I need you to take a message back to the queen."

When Nottie got the directions he left with five hundred men, "May God travel with you and keep you safe." Diego rode next to his son.

"As soon as we get the people to safety we will return," Nottie assured his father.

"Depending on how long it takes you to get back to the city with the villagers and farmers."

Riding on Nottie's other side Fredrex was tightening the buckle on his chain mail as he spoke "Ashes wants you to make sure that no one is left behind and see to it that the crops are torched. The flames and the smoke will keep any of Libbor's scouts from spotting you."

"I understand the king's reasons but it still seems a shame to waste so much food." Turning his horse's head, Nottie trotted off to join the men he was leading to search for the survivors.

As the two columns went their separate ways, Ashes was giving Thunk a message for Summer, and giving him orders.

"You're sure that you will be alright on your own?" Ashes asked, despite what the healer said Thunk insisted that the wounds that he had gotten in the battle with Libbor's men were minor.

Thunk sat on a fresh horse, a long-legged bay mare with a wild look to her eyes. Leaving his horse in the healer's care.

"I will be able to travel faster Alone my king." He patted the mare's shoulder, as he spoke, the mare was prancing in place; every muscle in her body trembling with eagerness "Babe is the fastest horse in your service and one rider will be less likely to be seen by any of Libbor's scouts. We will get your message to the queen."

"Here then, is the message I want you to give the queen." Ashes handed Thunk a small cylinder with a silver chain attached to it. Thunk put it around his neck and safely under the chain mail covering his chest. "Everything that she needs to know is there. She will know what needs to be done."

"It will be as you say, my King." Thrum relaxed the reins in his hand and Babe shot forward. Ashes watched them gallop off then he turned China and trotted back to the head of the column.

They traveled the rest of the day keeping a sharp eye out for any sign of Libbor's spies or scouts. That night they camped on top of a large hill top and posted guards. Diego just finished giving the guards their orders when Ashes approached him. "I told the men that cooking fires would be alright as long as the fires were small."

Ashes shrugged, "I am sure that Libbor's scouts know where we are anyway, so having fires won't hurt anything, but I think that it would be a good idea to rotate the men's sleep. I want half the men to be alert and ready, at all times. We don't need any surprises."

As Ashes spoke, he thought of the many times before, in his other past, that a war had been lost because a leader had got careless about such things. "His other past," the thought seemed so strange to him. Which one was real? Was this reality? And what he had thought was real a dream? Or was this a dream and he was still asleep in a desert? Or was this what the jewel had promised? His wish coming true? If this was his wish it was coming true in a strange way.

A slap on Ashes' shoulder interrupted his thoughts. "I asked you if you were hungry," Fredrex said, "I don't know about you but riding all day makes me hungry."

"Everything makes you hungry." Ashes pushed past his friend. "I swear that I always thought that if you were stuck somewhere with no food you would eat yourself."

Diego joined in laughing at the big man. "That's true enough." Jerking a thumb at Fredrex, he went on. "When we were in the high mountains last year, I saw this dolt try to eat a whole rack of bear ribs by himself."

"It's wrong to waste food." Fredrex said indignantly. "We killed the bear. It is only right that we honor its life by not letting its death be for nothing. If it was the other way around I would hope that the bear showed me the same respect."

Shaking his head, Ashes walked away from the two men. "Fredrex you are the only person I know that would think that being eaten by a hungry bear was a respectful end."

Arguing, good naturedly, the two men followed Ashes toward the main tent. The main tent was a large grey tent that was big enough for a makeshift table with a map, and another table full of fruit and meat. There was plenty of room for the three and for the men already gathered around the map deep in discussion.

The talk quieted down, as Ashes walked in. "Sire, we were just discussing what Libbor's next move might be."

Like the other men in the tent, the one who spoke was dressed in chainmail and had twin swords across his back. Vale, Fredrex's older brother. He was the oldest man in the room. His hair was more grey than the once black that it used to be.

Ashes crossed over to the table pausing to cut a slice of meat off of a still smoking roast. He had a choice of burnt or raw. The irony almost made him laugh out loud, the best soldiers in any kingdom and not one of them could cook.

Chewing on the meat, Ashes joined the other men, around the map, Vale went on as Ashes studied the map." Scouts have reported that Libbor's men are encamped at Spiral Valley. It makes little sense, that is a very poor place for a base camp and they could travel further into our territories with no resistance but they are not. The scouts think that they might be waiting for something"

"I agree." Ashes said softly, "Reinforcements, maybe? They know now, that we know they are here. They could be waiting for more men."

A much younger man standing just behind Vale spoke up " we could still burn the bridge, Or with luck two or three men could sneak past their scouts and guards in the dark, if they worked quickly they could cut the main supports on the bridge, without them the bridge would collapse."

Sighing, Vale ran his hand through his hair. "There are two things wrong with your idea Clip. First, the main supports on that bridge are woven from ironwood vines, and are over two feet thick, a man could hack away all day and not get halfway through them and second, destroying the bridge now would not only cut off their reinforcements and supplies, but it would also cut off their only way home."

Using his finger Vale traced along the map. "Thunder Gorge runs from Black Tooth Cliffs which there is no way over, to the Northern Sea and at this time of year no ship in existence could navigate the cross-tides over the Red Shoals. That leaves only the bridge, and if we destroy that, they are trapped! Their only choice would be to surrender or die, and the last time that one of Libbor's generals surrendered to a foe. Libbor had the entire company of men and their families burned alive as a warning."

"That is unfortunate." Clip said with an edge of sarcasm in his voice. "But they are trying to kill us, and our families. We need to do what we have to do, to keep that from happening." Seeing the flash of anger in Vale's eyes, Ashes spoke quickly to stop the argument.

"That is one way of looking at it Clip, but consider this. Even if they are our enemy, I am not sure that all of them want to be here. Libbor will drag anyone that he can into his armies. Farmers, miners -- whoever he can get his hands on, and they have families, their hearts are not in this war. If it starts to go bad for them, then they will most likely retreat. If we cut off that retreat and they know what Libbor will do to them and their families, if they surrender, then they will feel that they have no choice. Men who feel that they have nothing to lose are

the most dangerous kind, Clip. If we leave them a way home they will take it"
On the second day after Ashes left with the troops the first people from the countryside started arriving in small groups. Since then, more and more people had shown up, bringing with them their most prized possessions. Summer had been very busy trying to make sure that things went smoothly getting them settled in their temporary homes. Most things went well with very few problems.

Summer was very proud of the citizens who opened their homes to those who had lost theirs, but still, more people came. Summer started to house some people in the empty barracks but that was a temporary solution, at best, till the soldiers returned. There was no way of knowing how long it would be before the people could return to their homes, and to the lives that they had left behind.

Summer walked down the main road of the city; with her was Abby and Noel the city overseer. Also with her was her nephew Blueberry, a name that most who did not know his story would wonder about, having been born early he had always been small, the healers had been surprised that he had even lived his first week but even though his body was small his will to live even then, was huge. He survived his first week and the many bouts of illness that plagued him in his young life, proving to be far stronger than anyone thought.

Just after his second birthday he fell very ill, and nothing the healers did seemed to be working. His parents refused to give up on him. In desperation, his mother wrapped him in his favorite blanket, a heavy old blue one his grandfather had given him. The blanket was both worn and old but the boy loved it. His mother stayed by his side all that night praying for her son's life. In the morning when his father entered the room, the child's father found his wife, sleeping with her arms tightly hugging their son. The illness had passed, never to bother the boy again. When telling the story, his father had always joked that it looked like she was squeezing the juice out of a "blueberry." The name stuck.

This was Blueberry's twenty-first year of life. Having beaten the illness he had grown into a handsome young man that despite his smaller size turned many a woman's head. Blueberry's dreams, of fighting alongside his father, would never be. Ashes had decided that it would not be right to put him in battle against much larger men where he would have little chance. So when Blueberry became old enough he was given the job of advisor to the court, a job that was usually given to a much older person. Some had questioned the decision, but even though being disappointed at not becoming a warrior, he had taken to the job of advisor very well, impressing even his strongest critics.

Blueberry walked beside Summer, having to take longer steps to keep up with her pace. "All of the barracks are full and more people are still coming in. my queen. There are a few empty warehouses next to the South wall but they are cold and drafty, I think we should only use them as a last resort."

"I agree," Noel put in, "but we are running out of room Nottie just arrived with over three hundred more villagers we are going to be hard pressed to find suitable places for them to live."

Noel had to do a quick side-step to avoid being struck by a wooden sword being swung by one of two young boys play-fighting in the street.

The boy looked up sheepishly from the imagined battle. "Sorry queen Summer, sorry sir, I did not see you there."

"No harm done," Noel told the boy. "But maybe you should go over to the grove to play, so that you don't accidentally get run over by a wagon. The streets are very busy today." Nodding, the boy gave Summer a shy smile before heading off at a run in the direction of the grove, as Summer watched the two boys running toward the trees. She looked thoughtfully at the castle sitting on the other side of the large grove.

"Why not put the people in the west hall?"
She asked. All three of her companions
turned to follow her gaze,

"It could work." Blueberry agreed. "It is
empty, and there is plenty of room. It even
has a dining hall and furnishings.

"Good then," Summer said, satisfied. "I
will leave it to you to take care of it"

Summer spent the rest of the day,
checking to make sure that there were no
new problems, before heading back to her
and Ashes' chambers. In the castle. She
was tired both mentally and physically. She
was looking forward to the bath that the
chambermaid had drawn. She had just
pulled off her boots when she was
interrupted by a knock at the door. "Forgive
me my queen," an apologetic voice said,"
but a rider has arrived with a message from
the King."

Summer got up quickly, sighing, her bath
would have to wait.

"Is he in the hall?" Summer asked,
starting to pull her boots back on.

"No my lady, he said it was most
important that he speak to you as soon as
possible. He is with me.

"Glancing longingly at the bath," Summer
said, "Let him in."

As the newcomer entered the room,
Summer finished pulling on her boots. "I
am sorry to interrupt your evening my Lady
but I promised the King that I would give

you his message as soon as I reached the city."

Summer rose, smiling at the man.

"You interrupted nothing important, what is the message my husband sent?"

Thunk lifted the small silver chain and its container over his head and handed it to Summer then he waited in silence as Summer opened the small tube and smoothed out the tightly wrapped paper tilting it into the candle light to read it better.

A look of surprise showed briefly in her eyes passing quickly. Setting the note on the table next to her, she turned back to think." You have not eaten or rested, since you got back?"

Thunk shook his head, "No my Lady. As I said, I promised the king..."

That you would bring the message to me as soon as you arrived." Summer interrupted "and you have, thank you." Summer paused, hesitating before asking, "Did the king tell you what the message said?"

Again Thunk shook his head, "No my lady he only asked me to bring it to you."

Summer glanced back down at the paper, "And no one else knows about this?"

Thunk thought for a moment. "I only talked to the guards at the palace doors and the chambermaid my Lady, is there a problem?"

Summer chuckled softly, "Besides a war you mean?"

Thunk's face reddened, embarrassed.

Summer smiled, putting a gentle hand on the man's shoulder, "Forgive me, I was not trying to make you feel foolish. I must ask you to do one more thing, you know Abby and Noel?"

"Of course, my Lady," came the answer.

Nodding Summer went on, "Good, find them both and tell them I need to see them immediately. Then eat and get some sleep you have more than earned it."

Summer waited till Thunk left the room before picking up the paper and reading it again, mumbling softly to herself, "My husband, do you really think this is necessary? I don't even know if we can find them."

The look on both Abby's and Noel's face showed the same doubt that Summer had felt, "Are you sure that is what he said?" Noel asked, shocked, as Abby paced the room in frustration."

"He wants us to ask the Cocoans for help?"

Summer arched an eyebrow. "Are you doubting my ability to read?"

"No one has seen any sign of them in ten years, they are nomads! They disappeared into those mountains like ticks on a dog!" Abby shot before Noel could answer.

"We don't even know for sure where they are, or if they will help, they don't like people bothering them. They made that clear the last time we went looking for them!"

"True." Summer agreed. "But they would not even have survived, if we had not helped them cure the illness that was killing them off by the hundreds, and had Ashes not given them a quarter of our Kingdom to start a new life on, after we found that the sickness came from the waters in their own lands."

"Yes," Noel said. "But Ashes only gave them that land after they flat out refused his offer to join with us as one people. They do not like people other than themselves. The reason that they have not attacked us is because Ravage, their leader, knows what they owe us. That does not mean that he likes us."

"I am sure that Ashes has already thought about that." Summer said walking over to the tub, by the wall. She stuck her hand into the, now, cold bath water.

"But I also know he would not ask us to risk this, if he did not think it was necessary."

"Abby, I want you to send ten of your most trusted guardsmen to look for them in the morning. I will send the royal seal with them so Ravage knows that they speak for the king. They are to tell no one where they are going or why. Make sure that they know that. If Ravage and his people chose to help us we will welcome them as friends and allies, if not we will fight this war alone."

Summer pulled her hand out of the tub and flicked the cold water from her hand. "Tell only the men you send about this. Neither of you are to say anything to anyone else." She paused and then said, "Thank you both of you for coming, go get some sleep."

Waiting till she was alone Summer closed the chamber door, and walked to the table to read Ashes message again. Then she crossed the room to sit on the large bed and she did something she had not done in many months... Summer prayed.

CHAPTER 7
War

The night passed slowly for Ashes, a veteran of many wars, he usually had no trouble sleeping. This night though, sleep came grudgingly. It seemed that he had just closed his eyes when Fredrex pushed his head inside the tent and woke him. Looking past his friend, Ashes could see the soft light of early morning.

"The men are breaking camp Sire. We will be ready to march before daylight." Ashes rolled out of his blankets he was fully dressed except for his chain mail that was in a pile at the foot of his bedroll."

"Any trouble last night? Any sign of any of Libbor's scouts?"

"No Sire, everything was quiet. Nothing has changed. Our scouts have reported that Libbor is still camped at Spiral Valley. Not sure if that is good or bad."

"Huh." Ashes grunted. He was not a morning person, a fact that Summer, had pointed out many times.

"You want something to help you wake up?" Fredrex asked.

Ashes glared at the big man not sure if he was being friendly or sarcastic.

Picking up his chain mail, Ashes pushed past his friend. "What I need is for you to get your ass out of my way. I need to take a piss and you are the one thing stopping me."

Giving a deep mock bow, Fredrex stepped aside. "As you wish, my king. Should I get one of the men to assist you?"

"Kindly go to hell." Ashes muttered over his shoulder as he headed for the nearest trees.

By daylight, they had left their camp behind, and they were moving towards Spiral Valley. And Libbor's army, by midday the valley was in sight as was Libbor's camp. Ashes reined in China at the top of a rise. Studying the situation, Fredrex and Diego pulled their horses up beside him. The rest of the column halted just out of sight of Libbor's camp.

"I want to talk to Libbor myself before we do anything else. Send a rider with a white flag to tell Libbor that I will meet him and the other kings at the bottom of the valley."

"He won't listen to anything that you say," Diego protested. "And you will be taking a very big risk that he won't try to have you killed right there."

Ashes smiled thinly at the other man. "Oh I am sure he won't listen, but I have to try. I will not throw away so many lives on both sides if it can be avoided,"

Ashes laughed softly as he went on. "And as far as him trying to have me killed, why, that is why I will have my best friends beside me. To throw yourselves in front of any arrows that come my way."

From the top of the rise, they watched the messenger ride toward Libbor's camp. A small group of men rode out to meet him. Ashes watched, tensely waiting to see what the other riders were going to do. It took a man with true courage to do such a thing Ashes thought, when this was over he would see to it that the messenger was well rewarded for his bravery.

The group of riders formed a circle around the rider. Ashes could see them talking. After a moment, one of them galloped his horse back to their camp. A short while later, he returned to the small group. And he could see the men talking to the messenger. Then the circle of men headed back to their camp letting the messenger return the way he had come.

The man rode up to Ashes and the others. "Libbor said he would meet you, my king, but only you and him -- no one else. He said he will not put all of their leaders' lives at risk. It has to be just you and him."

"He invades our lands, kills our people without cause, and questions our honor." Fredrex growled. "I don't trust this. Sire, who is to say he will not have an archer hiding somewhere to kill you the moment you get in range? The man has proved time and time again that he is not to be trusted!"

"No, he is not to be trusted," Ashes agreed. "But he is not going to put his own life in danger. He knows that our archers are better than his. He would never make it back to his own camp if he tried anything like that, and he knows it!"

As Ashes spoke, he could see Libbor on horseback, waiting at the edge of his camp. Ashes nudged China forward into the valley. Ashes got to the meeting place first and waited as Libbor rode toward him reining in his horse ten feet away.

Libbor was a big man heavily muscled and scarred. His blonde beard covered most of his face, and his hair fell to his shoulders. He was in his thirties and had spent twenty years of them fighting in one war or another. Ashes knew that this man enjoyed causing others pain. He had heard him brag more than once about how slowly he had killed a foe. Ashes also knew that one day he would have to kill this man. Something that he was not going to enjoy, but neither was he going to regret it.

"What do you want Ashes? Are you here to try to talk me into just going home? Or have you grown so weak and old that just the sight of another army frightens you? Do you think that I will feel pity on you and your people and spare you?"

"I am here to try to talk some sense into you Libbor." Ashes tried not to let the contempt he was feeling for this man show in his voice "A war will cause nothing but pain and death on both sides. Winter is only a few months away children will need their fathers and wives will need their husbands. It is a foolish king who throws his soldier's lives away and put his people at risk."

Sneering Libbor used one hand to gesture behind him. "Does it look like I am the one throwing his men's lives away, fool? Look hard! Ashes, see your kingdom's end. I have fifteen thousand men now, and seven thousand more on their way. I know that you have -- at best --five thousand men. I don't think it is I who will be throwing his men's lives away!"

"You sit in your city, like a god, above everyone else. Behind your marble walls, looking down the other lands, handing out favors and gifts when you see fit, to those of us who come begging and are willing to bow down to you."

"You think that you are untouchable, with your great army. You are wrong! We will not ask or beg for what we need from you old fool, we will take it!

Four kingdoms have joined together against you to drag you off your throne and burn your city. You stand alone, Ashes, you will fight, but you will fail. Your lands will be ours!" Libbor's sneer broadened. "And your queen will be mine!"

Ashes had to fight hard to stop himself from attacking Libbor. He knew that, despite Libbor's size, of the two, he was the better fighter. He had no doubt that he could kill Libbor in a battle. But not right this moment. "Later." He thought. "There will be another time -- but not now."

"I have never made you, or anyone else, beg for anything Libbor. You have never been turned away. No matter what you asked. If you were sane, you would know that, but you are beyond reason. I had hoped otherwise, for the sake of your men, I will say this one time. Leave! Go back to your lands and we will not take revenge on you for the deaths of the people in the village, but if you wish a war then you will end up regretting it. Numbers do not mean victory Libbor. You will learn that!"

Ashes could feel China tense under him. The stallion could sense the tension in the air between the two men and knew what was coming. Every muscle in his powerful body waiting for the signal from his rider that would send him slamming into the other stallion. Ashes patted China's withers. "Not yet my friend." The touch said, "Very soon but not just yet." Feeling a gentle tug on the reins and a nudge in his side China reluctantly turned and headed back up the hill.

Ashes half-expected to feel an arrow in the back as he rode back to his men. Knowing Libbor was not beyond such a thing, but Ashes knew that Libbor also knew that his own men were watching and ready. If such a thing were to happen neither man would survive this meeting. Confident in his men, he rode back to at an easy trot.

Fredrex and Diego met him at the top of the rise. "I take it that things went as we thought they would?" Diego grunted. "The fool would not listen to reason?

Keeping China at a trot, Ashes ordered, "Ready the men and send for Vale. Libbor wants a war and nothing is going to change that, there is no point in waiting for his reinforcements to get here."

As Diego spurred his horse ahead to find Vale and give him the message, Ashes went on "Libbor brags that he has seven thousand more men on the way. He did not say how far away they are and we do not know if that is true but we are not going to take the chance. We will leave Vale behind with a thousand men. They can watch our flank and if need be, will act as our reinforcements."

Vale and Diego met them at the top of the rise and Ashes repeated his orders to Vale. "We will be ready and waiting if you need us my king," Vale promised. "And if Libbor's reinforcements get here, we will make them wish that they had stayed on their own side of the gorge."

Zlarora's troops were known as the best trained, in all of the kingdoms. Even Ashes was impressed with the speed in which the men moved into position. Every man was ready, knowing what was expected of him. He felt a burst of pride in them. Along with a deep sorrow, knowing that not all of these men were going to see their homes again. In wars, both sides lose men. Even in the best.

In the fading light, he could see the confusion in the other camp, as Libbor's men ran out of their tents and raced for their horses. Even at this distance Ashes could hear yelled orders being given as surprised officers tried to ready their men. Ashes men and horses had traveled all day. Libbor had counted on them being weary from the journey.

Ashes' army's readiness was the one thing that Libbor had not expected. Libbor had badly underestimated his opponents.

A night attack was rare. It was hard enough in a battle in the daylight to keep track of who your friend or foe was. In the dark, it was much worse. Mistakes could be made. Ashes was counting on that. He knew his men were trained in such things. Libbor's men were not. They would be confused and would be swinging at anyone they thought was an enemy. In the dark, in a crowded battle, superior numbers were a liability.

Ashes drew his sword raising it high in the air, China rearing under him. Ashes barely heard the trumpets sound on both sides of him, as forelegs, still churning in the air, China lunged forward and the air was filled with the thunder of thousands of hooves striking the ground, as a solid wall of men and horses rode into the valley toward their enemies.

CHAPTER 8
Sometimes, Even the Best Must Retreat

Arrows, from the enemy camp, rained down on them, as Libbor's men tried frantically to mount a defense. Most of the arrows bounced harmlessly off of both men's and horses' armor and shields, but some of the arrows found their mark.

Several of Ashes men and horses went down in the charge. Even caught by surprise, Libbor's men were able to meet the charge with a line of their own riders. The two lines collided less than a hundred feet from the outskirts of Libbor's camp.

Two riders were coming up fast, on either side of Ashes, he felt the shock all the way up his arm as he swung his shield around to knock the closest one off his horse. The man flew off of his horse and disappeared beneath a wall of horse hooves. The second rider took advantage of the opening and tried to separate Ashes' head from his body. Ashes brought up an armored arm to block the swing and shoved his own sword through the man's unprotected neck.

China stumbled sideways, as another rider drove his horse into his side trying to knock him over. Ashes had to shift his weight quickly as the stallion whirled around and planted both hind feet in two the other horse's shoulder. Both horse and rider went down.

Few things are more feared in a battle than a cavalry charge, a line of men and horses at full gallop can cut an army to pieces. When given the command a warhorse will rear on his hind legs to add its weight to the weight to that of its rider, giving the rider the weight of the horse as well as his own. Behind the swing of his sword, Zlarora's horses and riders worked together, very well. Many stories were told of when a rider went down either wounded or killed, his mount would continue the fight on his own protecting the rider's body.

The first battle lasted into the morning. When the sky lightened, the bodies of men and horses littered the valley floor, but neither side had gained any ground. Libbor's forces managed to rally enough to slow the charge, but they could not drive the Zlaroran army back, and the Zlarorans, even though they were better trained and armed, were simply too outnumbered.

All night long, Ashes had tried to find Libbor In the mass of horses and men, Ashes finally spotted Libbor in the first morning's light on the far edge of the valley watching the battle below." coward" he thought " come down here and fight with your men!"

He had hoped to put an end to this man, in the battle. Without him, the other leaders might have decided that they had had enough and leave with what men that they had left, but Libbor was not fool-enough to put himself at such risk, letting other men do the fighting and dying, while he stayed safe.

Diego charged his horse through the swirling confusion of men and horses, sliding to a stop beside him a bloody bandage was wrapped around one leg and blood was seeping through the side of his armor, "Ashes! Libbor's reinforcements are here. Vale has taken the rear guard to head them off."

A quick look around told Ashes what he needed to know. They were winning, but still heavily outnumbered and with Vale going to engage Libbor's reinforcements they had lost their reinforcements. It galled Ashes. He did not like the thought of letting Libbor think that he had won the battle, but too many bodies lay on the valley floor. If they continued this battle, here, there was little to be gained, "Sound the call to retreat!"

Diego started to protest then thought better of it. He gave Ashes a quick nod, and he spun his horse around and raced off to give the command. Ashes turned China to follow, stopping long enough to look over his shoulder. He could see Libbor watching him. "I promise that I will make you pay for every life lost, and for every foot of our land that you cross. This war will win you nothing but death."

Just watching the battle, from the valley rise was not what Vale wanted to be doing. He would far rather be fighting alongside of his king and companions. He knew the reason that Ashes had them held in reserve and he agreed with the reasoning behind his king's decision but that did little to ease the helplessness that he felt.

Vale could tell from the look on Clip's face that the younger warrior felt the same. "It is almost morning. So far the scouts have spotted no sign of the rest of Libbor's troops. We should ride down there and help our king put an end to this."

Vale's eyes never left the battle. "We stay here and do as we were ordered by our king. If they need us, they will signal us. Tell them that we wait and watch. Battles have been lost by foolish mistakes, and I do not intend to make one."

Clip did not comment on Vale's remark, but the older warrior knew that he had struck a nerve, and stirred up an old memory. Two years prior, Clip had been in charge of a patrol to pursue a group of thieves. Clip was young and overconfident.

He had charged the thieves camp, only to find that he and his men were vastly outnumbered. They had managed to get away with no casualties, but the thieves got away with the goods that they had stolen. Fredrex was not happy about it or about the way that the young warrior had handled things. Fredrex had made that very clear.

Vale had not intended to remind Clip of this failure, but he knew that even if he said so, the younger man would likely not believe him. At any rate, this was not the time to try to soothe hurt feelings.

"Something is up!" Clip was looking past Vale's shoulder, tracking two riders coming up fast. Clip and Value were showered with dirt, as the two riders brought their horses to a sliding stop. The horses were blowing hard and dripping sweat. Both men's armor was bloody and battered.

"Commander!" the closest one yelled after their horses had stopped.

"Libbor's reinforcements are coming. They are not two miles away, there are at least seven thousand men! We were ambushed by their scouts just after we saw them. Or we would have warned you sooner."

"You did well," Vale told the two men. "Go get your wounds tended to, and get fresh mounts. You may be needed!"

He gave Clip a thin smile. "Send word to Ashes of what is happening. I will ready the men. You wanted a battle my friend; looks like you are going to get one, maybe more than you wanted."

Vale took his men quickly, to head off Libbors reinforcements. They were less than a mile from the main battle when they found them. Vale never even slowed his horse when he gave the command to charge. Like his king, he knew that he was outnumbered. Also, like his king, he had great confidence in the men in his command.

Most of the front of the column of the reinforcements were riders and foot soldiers, with supply wagons bringing up the rear. Vale sent a squad of men to the rear to cut off the wagons from the rest of the column. "We will keep the others busy. The wagons are yours to deal with, Cut the horses loose and set the wagons on fire!"

Vale rode in, at a full charge, he could see Clip beside him riding a smallish mare named *Topper*. The name always struck Vale as funny. The little mare was very fast and agile. Every time that Clip had won a race, he had always bragged that no one could top her, hence her name.

As Clip pulled ahead, Vale, on his heavier horse, "Calico," a powerful stallion, fell behind the smaller mare. "Slow down you fool!" Vale's words were lost in the chaos of the charge.

They struck the column head on vale's troops spread out on both sides coming around in a half moon to trap the enemy. Pushing them in on themselves. Numbers were on the enemy's side, and Vale knew his best ally now was panic and confusion.

Clip was several lengths ahead of the others when he reached the column of men. The few arrows that came his way were poorly aimed, none coming close to him. He drew his swords. Trusting Topper to hold her course as he charged into the first of the riders. He was the best swordsmen in Ashes' army. The problem was, that he knew it.

The first riders that he met went down under his blades before they even got their guard up. Three more tried to box him in to bring him down. Topper sank her teeth into the closest man's leg dragging him off his horse. Fighting with both swords at once, Clip blocked a swing from one man using the momentum from the swing to help drive his sword into the other man's chest. Topper shoved her way through the other horses as Clip used a backhanded swing to knock the last man from his mount.

Neither man or horse saw the spear thrower before he shoved his spear deep into Topper's shoulder. Topper let out a squeal of rage and pain as she went down. Clip hit the ground hard. Rolling over several times before he stopped. He got to his feet quickly to see Topper trying to get her hooves back under her the spear-shaft broken off, in her shoulder, jutting out like a misshapen bone.

"No, Topper!" Clip's yell rose above the sound of the battle. He was beside the mare, in seconds, both fending off attacks and trying to help her to hooves. The mare shoved herself up onto three legs, and stood blowing hard, blood running thickly from her shoulder. As clip ran a worried hand across the mare's flank, he heard Vales yell. "Behind you, you fool!"

Even as Clip started to turn, he knew that it was too late. One of Libbors men was already swinging his axe. He only had time to bring his sword down. He managed to deflect the swing downwards away from his chest but not stopping it. The axe head severed his leg just below the knee.

Vale leaped over Clip as he fell to the ground and shoved his sword through the axe man's throat. Then turned on Clip. "Damn you for a fool! If he had not cut your leg out from under you I would have when this was over! Do! You! Ever! Learn!?"

Spotting two of their men close by, Vale yelled, to be heard over the battle, "Watch our backs while I tend to him!" The two moved in on either side as working quickly, Vale tore a strip of cloth off a nearby body and tied it around Clip's leg just above the knee. Shoving the broken spear shaft through, he twisted the makeshift bandage tight till the blood flow slowed and then stopped.

"Hold on to this." Vale grunted. Looking around, he spotted a torch still burning. Grabbing it, he blew on it until the flame burned hot. "Sorry about this pup, but it is the only sure way to keep you from bleeding to death." He placed the handle of his dagger to Clip's mouth. "Bite on this." Clip bit down just as Vale shoved the torch against the severed stump then Clip's vision went dark.

When he opened his eyes the air was filled with the smell of burnt flesh, and Clip saw Vale pulling the spear-shaft from Topper's shoulder. A third man was holding the mare's reins tight, keeping her head still. "Don't let her move" Vale said. Vale shoved the torch onto the mare's gaping wound. "This is going to make you mad mare."

Topper let out a squeal of anger, her ears pinned flat against her head as Vale brushed away the burnt hair to look at the wound. Satisfied, he grunted, "Going to leave one hell of a scar mare and you are going to have a limp, but you will live." Reaching down, Vale got an arm around Clip's shoulders and helped him to his one good foot. Clip staggered and leaned heavily on the other man for a second. "Do you think you can stay on your horse if we get you up there?"

Clip nodded weakly, "I will be ok, help me on and I can still fight."

"I used to think you kept your brain in your ass, now I know it was in your foot, pup, this fight is over for you and Topper. I admire bravery but stupidity is another thing." Despite his hard words, Vale was very gentle, as he helped the younger man on his mount. Clip's severed stump still seeped blood. Vale knew that it would not take much for the leg to break open again and if that happened Clip would surely bleed to death. Vale tore another strip of cloth from a body and despite Clip's protest tied the younger man's good leg tight, to the saddle, to keep him in place.

"How am I supposed to ride properly like this?!" Clip shot.

"You're not! In case you did not notice, some arrogant fool, in a foolish move cost you your leg and your mare damn near her life, be grateful that I don't tie you down like a sack of grain and have you ponied off, now get going! Go slow! We have your back. I will talk to you when this is over." Vale watched as glaring down at him Clip headed Topper away from the fighting, even limping badly, the mare was pulling at the bit. "Just like her rider," Vale mused, "sometimes too proud and too stubborn for her own good." As Vale had been tending to Clip's wounds the fighting had moved on.

Vale grabbed his sword and hurried to join the battle.

Ashes had expected Libbor's men to at least try to pursue them as they pulled back. A few arrows and spears came their way, but their foes seemed to have little interest in continuing the fight. "With good reason" Ashes thought. The valley was littered with enemy bodies.

With Diego riding beside him, they headed out of the valley. "I am going to take some men and help Vale. You stay here and keep an eye on Libbor's troops. I don't think that they will do anything right now but be ready."

Ashes did not wait for an answer before he spurred China to hurry faster and gather the men he needed. The men and horses were tired. He knew that, but they would have to wait a little longer to rest too many lives had been lost already.

The battle was over before they got there. The only proof that there had been a battle was the burning wagons and the bodies that were here and there. Most of Libbor's reinforcements had fled into the hills. Vale met them, as they rode up. "The fighting is over here we were just about to head back to help you, seeing as how you are here I take it the battle is over?"

"For now," Ashes answered, "we pulled back. Libbor chose not to pursue; this battle has cost him far more than it has us. Still, we need to regroup and see to the wounded and we need to make a plan. We won't need to worry about Libbor's men for a few days. Recall your men."

Taking off his helmet, Vale ran a hand through his hair. "Uhhh, there is one more thing. I am not sure how you want to deal with it." turning Calco, Vale called over his shoulder, "Come on, the men found something in one of the wagons that you should see."

A little annoyed by Vale's elusiveness Ashes followed, as Vale led them to a small group of people standing under a tree. Even before they got to them Ashes could see what Vale meant.

The women seemed to vary in age from their mid-teens to early forties, and varied in both height and weight, but they all had one thing in common. All of them were covered with cuts and bruises and all of them were wearing what once might have been dresses tied as best as they could around them. And all of them looked very frightened.

Ashes could not help the anger that he felt when he saw them. "They were tied and gagged in the last two wagons," Vale explained, "It was a good thing that the men looked inside before they burned the wagons."

Sliding out of his saddle, Ashes, walked closer to the women. Seeing the fear in their eyes he stopped. "You don't have to fear us, we are not going to harm you. Who are you? What land did Libbor take you from?"

The oldest of the women put herself between him and the others. "I am called Roxie. We come from different lands. Libbor's mercenaries killed our families and burned our homes weeks ago when we told them that we wanted no part of this war. They have been keeping us alive for his troops every since. We tried to fight them and escape -- more than once!" She looked around at the others. "You can see how we paid for our disobedience."

"To try, more than once, knowing what would happen to you, should you fail was brave." Fredrex swung down off his horse, as he spoke, "But you are safe now, as my king has said. You have nothing to fear from us."

Ashes had been studying the women thoughtfully as Roxie told their story. They all were scared, dirty, and worn; but they looked healthy. The cuts that marked them did not look life-threatening. Ashes tried to think of a way that he could help these women. "You said that you lost your homes?" Ashes asked.

Roxie nodded, so Ashes continued. "I could help you, either to return to your lands, when this war is over, or to start a new life here. We could use your help with the wounded, care for the horses, cook, help set up camp. There are a lot of things that you could do. That would be a great help to us. If you are willing, and I give you my word that no man in my service will touch you or even speak to you in a disrespectful way."

"You do not have to. If you don't want to, if you prefer, we will send you back to Zlarora when the next supply wagons get here. I will still see to it that you are taken care of, but if you do stay, I will give each of you a hundred gold weight, when the war is over and a plot of land to start a new home."

Ashes walked from woman to woman, as he was talking, trying to ease their fears. He could see both the hope and uncertainty in their eyes. They had been treated worse than slaves by Libbor's men. And Ashes knew it was a hard thing to ask them to trust him.

A second woman stepped forward, dipping her head to him as she spoke. "I am Shamrock. My home was at the base of the Cheto Mountains far from here, but even there we heard the stories of Zlarora and its great king. We heard that he was a good man who cared for all his people. My home was burned -- like the others -- it is no more. My family is dead. I have nothing to return to. I will take your offer."

Lifting her head, she brushed a hand at her dirty red hair as it fell across her shoulders. "If you will allow first I would like to wash and try to mend my clothes"

One by one the other women all accepted Ashes' offer. "Take them back to the supply wagons. Let them rest, and give them whatever they need. Make sure that you tell the men to mind their manners not even a joke, these women have been through enough! "

Ashes was in a foul mood. The snow came early, and with it the cold. A month had passed since Ashes had first found the jewel, three weeks since the first battle with Libbor's armies yet it seemed like years. They had slowed their enemy advance to a crawl but they could not stop them. No matter how many of Libbor's men they killed in battle, there seemed to be more to replace them and while their losses were far less than Libbor's the losses were still telling.

Ashes sat in a farmhouse that they had made a camp around. Zloara was still a day's ride away but that was still far too close, and he was having a very hard time not giving in to his anger at the fact that Libbor had laid claim to their lands.

Telling the others that he wanted to be left alone, Ashes closed himself up in one of the rooms taking his saddle bags with him.

Looking to make sure no one else was in the room, he sat the bags on the table and opened the flap.

Even in the daylight, Ashes could see the glow coming from the gem. Reaching to take it out of the bag, he thought again of the day that he found it. Was that life a dream or was this one? Staring into the gem, he could see his own reflection on its surface taunting him.

"You promised me anything that I wished for, I asked for peace. I have seen nothing but war since I found you! Too many have died because of my wish! Why are you doing this? What am I doing wrong? Tell me -- damn you! How Do stop the killing?!" Silence answered him. "Did you really think that it was going to answer you?" He thought bitterly, still holding the jewel, he stared out the window at the tents and campfires glowing in the dim light he could see men huddled around the fires to keep warm.

A cold breeze blew through the window, past his ear. "These are your people, they knew what could happen when this started and they trust you. They would follow you into hell. You have to trust them! Nothing comes without a price -- not even peace!"

A knock at the door startled him looking around, he saw Fredrex standing in the doorway behind him. Shamrock was waiting with a tray of food. Fredrex entered the room and stood to one side, as Shamrock put the tray on the table. "You should eat sire." None of the women that they had rescued had left. They had all chosen to stay and help. Ashes was grateful for that. He thanked her, as she left the room.

"If I might have a word with you sire?" Fredrex ask, nodding Ashes walked to the table, and he sat the jewel next to the saddle bag. Fredrex crossed over to the table. "May I?," he asked, Ashes nodded again and watched closely as Fredrex reached down and picked up the jewel to study it.

"Not the first time that I saw you with this thing. Where did you get it? I have never seen anything like it; it is not a diamond or an emerald. Still beautiful, though. A gift for the queen?"

"Yes." Ashes lied. His friend would think him insane if he told him the truth. "I meant to give it to her before we left. I found it in a stream in the valley below the North wall. She loves shiny things."

Laughing, Fredrex tossed the jewel back to Ashes. "You had best hope that she never hears that you said that. I don't think that you will like where she puts it."

Fredrex laughter lifted Ashes spirits. He put the jewel back into the bags and buckled them shut. "You need something?"

The smile left Fredrex's face. "Yes, Ashes we need to talk, I know how you feel about

running from Libbor. I feel the same way --
all of us do. These men would fight and die,
to the last man, if you asked them to, but it
is wrong to throw their lives away."

Anger flashed in Ashes eyes. "If you think
that I don't care about these men's lives!!"

Fredrex put up a hand "I am not saying
that you don't care, or that you are doing
that now, what I am saying is that fighting
in the open is costing us."

"Ashes turned back to stare out the
window, as Fredrex went on." It is harder
on the men and the horses. Zlarora is only
a day's ride away. If we pulled back to the
city, we could rest and recover. There is no
way that Libbor's army could breach her
walls. Let the fool think he has gained
something. He will think different in a
month when the real cold hits, and his
supplies are low." Fredrex crossed the room
to stand next to Ashes, and looked out the
window.

"I have seen Libbor's catapults," Ashes
said, "They may not have them here, now,
but they can build them. The catapults are
self-loading and fast; not a lot of range, or
very heavily load. They would have to get
within arrow shot if they wanted to strike
past the city walls, but enough hits would
take its toll. The walls are marble... ten feet
thick... the gate is not! As strong as ironwood
is, it wouldn't take a barrage like that
forever."

Fredrex scratched, at a healing gash, on the side of his neck. Ashes remembered when Fredrex had gotten the gash. Fredrex had been dragging one of his men out from under a fallen foe and did not see when a man that he thought was dead lunged with a dagger. Had the lunge been two inches closer, Fredrex would not be here beside him now.

"It won't have to," Fredrex said, "Zlarora catapults may be old but they stand ready if needed and the city is not defenseless. Let the men see their homes again Ashes and let them be with their families. The farmers and villagers are safe now, there is no real need to continue the fight in the open."

"He is right." Ashes thought. "It is time to go home," nodding at Fredrex. "Alright tell the men, in the morning that we ride for Zlarora."

Fredrex started out the door, to give the order then stopped, as Vale stepped into the room, with a man behind him. Both Ashes and Fredrex stared in surprise at the newcomer, Casper, the King of the Hillibs.

Casper was as big as Fredrex and covered with scars. Both of his ears were cauliflowered and his nose sat crooked on his face having been broken many times. His shoulder-length brown hair was thinning. But the man carried himself with pride. Ashes noticed that he still had his sword.

"He rode in with some of his men, just now." Vale said, "He said that it was important that he talk to you so I brought him here."

Casper stepped forward. "I am not here as an enemy Ashes I come with news, if you will listen to it."

Ashes sat on the table next to the saddle bag." I will listen to what you have to say but know this, if this is a trick, you will not leave this room, under your own power."

Casper nodded, "Fair enough. I will be brief. I am leaving with my men Ashes, we are going home. Too many of us have died for Libbor's greed -- we will lose no more."

Fredrex gave the other man a questioning look. "And Libbor had nothing to say about this?" Casper's eyes darkened "Libbor can go to hell -- for all I care! The only reason we joined forces with him in this war, was because of his veiled threats. We are a small, landlocked country. Without trade we would starve. And Libbor's lands border us on three sides. I don't bear you, nor your people, any ill will Ashes, but I have to think of my own people. I did what I thought was best for them."

Vale snorted, "And how much of our lands did Libbor promise you? Or would you have us think otherwise."

Casper gave Vale a hard stare before answering. "I made no claim otherwise.

Much was promised if we joined in this foolishness and at the time I believed that I was doing the right thing for my people. I know now that it was a mistake."

We joined with three thousand men. Now, we are less than half that number. My men and I want nothing more than to return home. Grant us safe passage, and we will leave your lands."

Ashes picked up one of the mugs that Shamrock brought in, and handed it to Casper. "Half your men remain?"

Taking the mug from Ashes hand, Casper nodded. "We number just over thirteen hundred now and about seventy-five of them probably won't survive the trip home, maybe more. Libbor knew that the only way to stop us from leaving was a battle and he cannot afford to lose any more men but he did keep us from taking any supplies. We left with only what our horses can carry, and it is a very long journey."

Drinking from his own mug, Ashes thought for a moment, before looking over at Diego, "There are seven fully-loaded supply wagons now, Right?"

Diego did not even have to think before answering, "Just under seven."

Taking another drink, Ashes turned back to Casper. "Where are your men now?"

Casper drained his own mug and sat it on the table. "I did not trust Libbor; not to attack as we slept. I sent them ahead. They were about twenty miles north of here when I left them. Further away by now."

Ashes asked, "It will take you, what? Ten days, to return to your lands?"

Again, Casper nodded agreement. Ashes went on. "We will give you three supply wagons for your journey. Do you have men, here, to drive the wagons?"

Diego answered the question for Casper, "There are six men with him. They are in the other room, waiting."

"Good..." Ashes started to say, before Casper interrupted him.

"I did not come here to beg for favors Ashes, we do not need your charity! We will make the trip on our own!"

"Don't prove yourself a bigger fool, than you already have, when you joined this war!" Ashes shot back, at the other man. "Pride means nothing to a dead man, you said you lost half your men in the fighting. You will lose the other half trying to get home without supplies. A starving man has little chance in the cold, a wounded and starving man has no chance! But make no mistake about it Casper, we are giving you this for two reasons."

Ashes sat his mug down hard on the table and picked up the dagger he used to cut the meat and ran the tip across the table top "First, by your own admittance, many of your men are tired and wounded. Without supplies, they would very soon be weak from hunger. Hungry and weak men travel slowly, and I want you out of my lands as fast as possible; and second," Ashes' voice softened, "If it helps your pride, think of this as an exchange of goods. I have never given any thought to your country as a trading-partner in the past. Perhaps, if I had we both would not be here today," Ashes went on grudgingly, "when this is over that will change. We will consider this as being the beginning of an alliance if you are willing."

Doubt showed in Casper's eyes, "I would like that very much Ashes but your people would have to travel through Libbor's lands to reach mine. I don't think he will allow that, after this."

"We will deal with that, when we come to it," Ashes told him "and at any rate, I don't think that anyone will have to worry about Libbor when this war is over."

Casper crossed the room and held out a hand to Ashes. "I will leave you to deal with Libbor. As I said, I am done with this war. By your leave, we will be going, you have my gratitude. Ashes, I wish you and your men luck."

"Safe journey," Ashes answered as Casper turned to gather up his men. Ashes spoke again, "Be warned Casper, I do this for the reasons that I said and I will honor my promise to you but if this is a trick if you rejoin Libbor in this fight I will take it that you do not want this alliance. If that happens then you chose to be our enemy, and we will respond as such."

When the sun rose, the next morning, the camp and the farmhouse were both empty. Ashes and his men were a distant line, in the hills, marching home to Zlarora.

CHAPTER 9
Siege

Despite all that they had been through, spirits were high. Everyone knew that the war was far from over but the thought of seeing home and family once more made the war seem small by comparison. Ashes rode in the lead of the column with Fredrex, Diego and Nottie who had rejoined them.

It had snowed the night before, and, as the sun rose the glare on the new snow made it difficult to see very far. Scouts rode on all sides to keep watch.

"At this pace if nothing slows us down we should be in Zlarora, before nightfall," Nottie told them.

Ashes only half heard the young warrior. His mind was fixed on the events of the night before. At the start of the war, Libbor had just over twenty-two thousand men.

Casper had said that at the beginning of the war that he had three thousand men and that he had suffered heavy losses. He had taken his remaining men; just over thirteen hundred and had left. The war had taken a heavy toll on Libbor's troops, as it was. How many men did Libbor have left?

It was hard to get an accurate count. When some of the scouts had snuck into Libbor's camp, they had found that many of the tents in Libbor's camps were empty, with the bodies from the past battles propped up around the fires or tied to trees to make the camps look bigger than they were.

Ashes did not envy the men whose job it was to put the bodies in place. Most of the men were superstitious about such things. Even with the cold preserving the bodies it was not a pleasant job; probably reserved for those who had stirred Libbor's ire.

There had to be a reason for Libbor to go to such extremes. Ashes badly wished that he knew for sure what Libbor's losses were and if they attacked Libbor now in an all or nothing battle, could they end this war here and now, without endangering the city by leading an enemy army to its gates?

Ashes let out a deep sigh. It was tempting, but without knowing for sure he would be putting -- not only the lives of his men and his own life at risk but he would be putting Zlarora -- and all of its people at risk as well. It was not worth the risk. Whether for good, or for bad it seemed that the winner of this war would be decided at Zlarora's gates.

As it was, Nottie was only slightly wrong in his estimate of when they would reach the city. The sun had not yet set when they reached the flat plains with its well-traveled road to the city. Even at this distance the city guards could be seen on the walls watching their approach.

The city's walls were lined with guardsmen men that was to be expected with a war going on, but the trumpets sounding from the city, and the riders charging out the gates with Abby in the lead, racing toward them was not.

"What in the hell are they doing?!" Diego asked, "Don't tell me that Abby can't remember what our banner looks like?!" A shout of alarm came from behind, before anyone could answer. Ashes turned in his saddle as one of the rear scouts raced up on a lathered horse steam blowing in the cold air from the horse's wide nostrils.

"Sire the enemy is behind us. They surprised us about five miles back. I am the only one who got away. The rest are dead!"

Ashes could see the line of men and horses, spread out, charging down the rise onto the plains.

Ashes cursed softly, Libbor had lost half of his army either in battle or by Casper leaving, but they were still badly outnumbered. Even with Abby's and the city guard's help; with Libbor's men coming at a full charge the odds were too much against them. He hated the thought of running away but more was at stake than his pride. Libbor's army was close. The city was closer, and Libbor was closing the gap!

Ashes turned China around, and raced back along the line of men and horses. "Get to the city! Move! We will finish this there! Go!!" China spun in place as horses charged past at a run toward the city gates throwing clumps of snow into the air. The enemy line was only a half mile away when the last of the supply wagons went by heading towards the city.

Abby reined Brian in beside him worry and anger in her eyes. "Come on, move it! I have archers on the walls to cover us, but that won't do us any good here. We are too far out!" After a quick look, to make sure that there were no stragglers, Ashes and Abby raced for the city gates.

Ashes did not need to look behind him to know how close Libbor's men were; the arrows striking into the ground around them and the growing thunder of charging horses hooves behind them told him that they had waited too long to make their run for the city they were quickly being overtaken.

Ashes was just starting to think that they would have to turn and meet their attacker's charge when the first volley of arrows from the city went over their heads.

A look over his shoulder showed him the chaos they were inflicting on the enemy.

The arrows were taking their toll, and now riderless horses collided with each other trying to avoid the ones behind them.

Ashes and Abby rode through the gates as a second volley of arrows followed the first. Then a third. He brought China to a sliding stop just inside the city gates, swinging out of the saddle before his stallion had come to complete stop. As the gates closed behind him he could see their enemy retreating back out of arrow range.

The ground was littered with the bodies of Libbor's men who led the charge. The walls of the courtyard echoed as the great doors slammed shut they could do nothing now but rest and wait.

The courtyard was crowded with men, horses, and wagons; all trying to get out of each others' way officers barked orders at men who handed the reins of their blowing horses to waiting young men not yet old enough to fight. Then raced upstairs to help reinforce the men on the wall.

Someone ran into Ashes as he was turning back around. Throwing their arms around his neck; even if blind, he would have known her touch.

"Ashes! Husband!" Summer muttered happily into his ear. "I missed you sooo much!"

Not caring who saw them or what anyone thought Ashes wrapped his arms around Summer breathing in the scent of her hair and feeling the warmth of her body. Pulling her toward him he gave her a gentle kiss.

"Ahem! This is all very touching," Abby put in, "but we are still under attack. You two might want to wait a bit, before you get too carried away." Reluctantly, the two separated.

Ashes jerked a thumb in Abby's direction. "I thought that I told you in my message to get rid of her while I was gone."

Taking Ashes' hand, Summer led the way back toward the castle. "I was going to, but then I thought that if we really want to drive Libbor and his men away we could just sneak her into their camp and have her sing for them."

Crossing her arms, Abby glared at the two, "Do you really think that this is the time for this? The war! Remember?!"

"Not an easy thing to forget Abby," Fredrex muttered. "But we broke the attack, we're safe inside the city walls for now. Let them have this."

Ashes handed China's reins to Abby. "And here, seeing as how you are heading to the stables with Brian anyway, will you take care of China for me?"

Still glaring, Abby snatched the reins out of Ashes' hands and she headed off in the direction of the stables with Brian and

China in tow. China followed hesitantly. Abby tugged at the reins. "Come on stud. Don't worry. I am not mad at you. It is your rider that is going to be sorry."

The meal sat heavily in Libbor's belly. Supplies were low and he had ordered that the food be rationed to one meal a day per man; himself included. That alone was enough to put him in a bad mood. On top of that, he had watched his troops retreat from the Zlarorans archers when they were so close to the gates the sight of which sent him into a rage which he had only recently gotten over. It was not supposed to be this way, he was supposed to be sitting in Zlarora's throne room with Ashes' head decorating the wall behind his throne. Glaring at his plate, he pondered the events of the last six weeks.

Everything had gone as Libbor had planned; at least, at first. Casper, Garth, and Banner had agreed to join in the attack on Zlarora. His main fear had been that Ashes would destroy the bridge before he could cross. That did not happen. Ashes had been a fool to let it remain. Whatever his reason. They had taken the first village easily and had made it many leagues into Ashes kingdom before Ashes had arrived with his armies. Ashes proved unpredictable attacking the very night that he had arrived.

Even weary from travel, and being vastly outnumbered, his troops had nearly won the battle the first night. But again Ashes did the unexpected retreating, even when his forces were winning the battle. Since then, it had become even harder to predict what the fool would do.

To make things worse that coward, Casper, had taken his own men and left. Casper had been the most reluctant to join in this war, but Libbor had thought that the promises of reward, in both land and in wealth, that Casper would receive, when Zlarora was defeated had won him over. It seemed that he was mistaken about Casper.

Not that Libbor had any intent of keeping any of those promises to Casper, or to the others; his promises were a means to an end. No more! Once Ashes and Zlarora were out of the way he would deal with them but, for now he needed them -- as much as that thought disgusted him.

To fuel his anger even more Casper had gone to Ashes to beg like a dog for safe passage home. Not only did Ashes grant it, he gave the coward the food and the supplies that he needed for him and his men to make the journey to their homeland.

Libbor had considered sending some men to ambush Casper, and take the supplies for themselves but he could not afford to lose any more men especially with the outcome of such a battle being uncertain.

Then, only two nights ago, he sent scouts to recon Ashes camp and the surrounding lands he had been sure that he could end this war with a surprise attack on Ashes camp. In one last battle, moving quickly at night. They planned to surround the camp before the enemy knew they were there trapping them. And attack from all sides -- at once but when he had gotten there with his army, they found an empty camp.

Again, Ashes had done the unexpected and pulled back to Zlarora and the safety of its walls to add to Libbor's problems his allies were starting to doubt if this war was worth the price -- even if they did win. It turned his stomach to have to deal with such cowards. Libbor vowed that when this war was over that he would deal with them as well.

Libbor had no intent of sharing the spoils of this war with anyone. A thin smile crossed his face. Once this war was over he would rid himself of the other kings. It was time that these lands were joined as one kingdom -- with one king, him!

Libbor had planned each move carefully, making sure that in each battle his troops took the least losses. It had been hard to do without raising suspicion. Most of the men that he lost were those that he had forced into his service. He had managed to keep his better trained, more valuable, men away from the worst of the fighting.

Libbor thoughts returned to his plans, "Once Zlarora fell, it would be their job to deal with what remained of his allies. But Casper's treachery and Ashes' unpredictability had put all of Libbor's plans in jeopardy.

The sound of footsteps, on the snow outside of his tent brought Libbor out of his thoughts. A cold wind filled the tent as the flap was pulled aside and Banner followed Garth into the tent.

"A messenger has just arrived." Garth told him, "The catapults are two days away. In this weather, it is the best they can do."

Libbor gave the Odean king a quick nod of greeting. He was the oldest of the leaders in their alliance at least twenty years older than Libbor. Banner was as close a Libbor could tell, around his own age of thirty-four give or take a few years. Both men's armor was scratched and dented and both men carried the healing wounds of recent battles.

"I am not sure what good the catapults are going to be," Banner muttered, '"They are going to have to be within arrow-range, to even reach the city walls or its gate; Closer, if we mean to try reach the city. It is five hundred feet from the inner walls to the closest building, and even our strongest catapult under the best conditions cannot hurl a load that far."

"I don't intend to try to hit the city or the walls with the catapults. That is not why I sent for them." Standing, Libbor walked past the two men as he talked. His companions followed him back outside the tent.

Gesturing at the city, Libbor went on, "The walls are over ten feet thick. They are solid marble. We would never be able to breach the wall. We could try to loose some fireballs at the men on the walls and hope to kill a few but chances are small that it would be anything more than a distraction. We still might when we are ready to take the city but alone it wouldn't be enough. "For now, the target will be the gates. Them, we can hurt. They may be ironwood and they may be thick but they will burn if we hit them with enough burning oil, they will weaken."

A gust of wind blew snow around the three men's feet. Garth pulled his cloak tighter around himself, "We all have visited the city at one time or another Libbor, and we all have seen those gates. They are fireproof and even if the oil did get them burning they would just put the fires out. It would take months and a great deal of oil to do enough damage to weaken them."

Libbor turned a cold smile on the two men, "We have months, as many as needed. That fool Ashes has trapped himself and his people inside of the city with only one way out. There are sixteen wagons of oil on their way here now and more will follow. Months or years, it makes no difference, Zlarora will fall!"

The next day brought colder winds with heavy clouds that left behind two feet of new snow on the ground, delaying the arrival of the catapults. In the city, the people rested and readied themselves for the siege to come.

Ashes stood on the boardwalk of the east wall watching Libbor's camp. It had been over a week since they had fallen back to the city. In that time, besides the first failed attack when they got here there had been nothing more than a few arrows shot over the walls.

Libbor was waiting for something. He had to know that there was no way that he could take the city with just the men he had. Or he would have attacked in force by now. It was doubtful that he had more reinforcements coming.

Ashes stepped aside to let a line of men go past on their way to relieve the guards who were on duty. The man in the lead gave Ashes a quick salute as they went by. "Morning, sire. How is the queen, this morning?"

"Still sleeping," Ashes told him grinning, "She spent the best part of the night pointing out all of the bad habits that I had picked up while I was on the trail. It seems that tossing my torn trousers her way and asking her to mend them, was not a good idea."

The guardsmen's laugh echoed through the courtyard. "You are a braver man than I, sire. I would sooner charge our enemy's camp unarmed, and naked; than face the queen's anger in full armor and both my swords in hand."

"Then you are also a wiser man than my husband as well, good guardsmen. His intelligence. Is sometimes like his manners; short-lived and quickly forgotten." Summers' sudden appearance surprised the guards, but Ashes had grown used to how silently the woman could move.

One thing that both impressed and annoyed him was that the women could show up without warning at the worst of times. Another thing about her that he had gotten used to. The guardsmen waited, uncertain of what to say.

"You had best get to your posts." Ashes told the men. "And keep a sharp eye out. Libbor is planning something. I am not sure what it is, but we need to be ready when he makes his move."

Grateful to be leaving, the guardsmen continued on their way to relieve their counterparts. Summer watched them leave making sure that they were out-of-hearing range before she turned her attention back to Ashes. "The riders that we sent looking for the Cocoans still have not reported back and with Libbor's army camped out on our doorstep they may not be able to."

"We have to trust in them." Ashes told her. "They are good men."

Summer nodded absently staring over the wall. "Are you alright?" Ashes asked with concern.

Summer turned to him and gave him a long look before answering. "Your side of the bed was empty when I woke. That was hours before sunrise. I thought that you might be tending to your needs but you did not come back. It has been the same every night since you returned. It is not this war that is troubling you. I know you too well husband to believe that. There is something more. Are you unhappy with me?"

Her question took Ashes by surprise. Reaching out for her, he gently pulled her against him.

"Why would I be angry with you? A man could not ask for a better wife. A little moody." He put in laughing. "And not very sympathetic when it comes to your kings worn trousers but I have grown used to your moods. I would not change anything about you, so no, there is nothing that you have done that is troubling me."

Summer wrapped her arms around Ashes. "Huh." she muttered, "I love you, as well, husband, but given the chance, there are many things I would change about you, starting with your god-awful sense of humor!"

Even through the chain mail and the padding Summer felt Ashes stiffen.

"Husband?" but Ashes was no longer looking at her staring hard over her shoulder at the hills, in the distance. "Your sense of humor, and your attention span..." Summer thought to herself, turning to follow his gaze.

Several guardsmen were also running toward them. The reason for their haste could be seen working its way down the hillside. Libbor's catapults had arrived!

The main attack came the next morning, with Libbor using the dark-of-night to move the catapults into position. It was just past midnight when the first fireball struck the walls of the city. The burning oil filled the early morning with smoke and flame. By the time that the sun rose the air was thick with black smoke.

The Zlaroran's aging catapults exchanged shots with Libbor's scoring several hits forcing the remaining ones to pull back out of range of the heavy more damaging loads but the oil drums being lighter could still reach the city walls and its wooden gates, and Libbor's men's aim was getting better. The gates had been fire-proofed, but even that would not hold up forever under the burning oil's hot flames.

The walls around the gates darkened with soot. As the fires burned and the flames lapped up and over the walls. That along with the arrows coming from the Enemies archers, made the job of trying to put out the flames all but impossible.

It was snowflake and blueberry who came up with an answer to the problem. After many failed attempts to put out the flames and more than one man getting badly burned. Ashes was beginning to think that they would lose the gate altogether.

Even the gate's fireproofing could only do so much under such heat. At the rate that it was burning they had three days at most. Ashes watched from the wall as the guards made another vain try at putting out the fire. Several men working together, dumped huge vats of water, over the wall, onto the burning gate.

Their efforts were rewarded with billowing smoke and scalding clouds of steam but try as they might they could not get enough water on the fire at one time to be effective. By the time the vats were refilled, the fire had regained everything that it had lost. They were losing the fight with a foe they could not touch.

Fredrex stood beside Ashes, watching as another burning barrel of oil struck the gate. The impact sent smoke and flames into the sky. The Zlaroran archers had managed to slow the catapults -- but not stop them.

The bodies of the men who had carelessly let themselves be seen were scattered in the snow, around the catapults. Their main challenge was learning how to stay hidden, as they armed the catapults.

"I know that it is not our best choice, Ashes." Fredrex told him. "But we may have no other choice than a direct assault on their catapults." Ashes had to agree that they had to do something quickly.

"What if there was a better way?"

Both men turned at to look at the newcomer who had spoken. Blueberry and Snowflake stood side by side behind them looking nervously at each other. "Well?" Ashes ask them "Go on, do you have an idea what we can do?"

Snowflake nodded at Blueberry shyly. "Blueberry thought of it," she murmured.

"Well, I had the idea, but Snowflake figured out how we could do it." Blueberry told them.

"What idea?!" Fredrex spouted "Out with it, before the gate burns down if you don't mind!"

Ashes put a hand on the big man's shoulder. "Let's hear your idea you two..."

"The fountain!" Blueberry stuttered. "We could use the fountain to put out the fires!"

Ashes and Fredrex gave each other a questioning look "The fountain?" Ashes asked Blueberry, "Blueberry the fountain is not running. The water is diverted in the winter so the culverts don't freeze."

"Yes!" Blueberry went on excitedly. "The water is diverted to the drainpipes back to the underground river that supplies the city with water!" but the pipes and ducts that the water runs through, back to the river run just under the walls right by the gate!"

Snowflake put in "don't you see? All we have to do is dig up the drain pipes and divert them to the wall gratings over the gate, that would put the fires out and they could throw as much burning oil as they want. It won't do them any good."

"That would work, wouldn't it?" Blueberry asked.

"Damn if it wouldn't." Ashes muttered. "How long would it take?" Ashes asked Fredrex.

Fredrex was already on the run calling over his shoulder "With enough men, we can do it before the sun sets. Good job you two!" He added slapping Blueberry between the shoulder blades as he went by almost knocking the much smaller man off of his feet.

The work took a little longer than expected. The frozen ground and the cold made getting the pipes out of the ground difficult. With more than one shattering raising concerns that they would not be able to reach the grates over the gate but fate was with them and by the time that the moon had fully risen the night sky was filled with clouds of billowing steam, as the fire went out under a steady wall of water.

Libbor's catapults threw several more burning barrels at the gate trying to restart the flames, but the burning oil was quickly washed away by the manmade waterfall.

The victory against the fire was brief and short-lived. After staying up most of the night to make sure that the threat to the gate was passed Ashes had just reached his bed chambers and was hoping to get a few hours of sleep. Summer lay asleep on the bed. The blankets gently rising and falling with her breathing. The warmth of the room made him sleepy as he watched the light from the fireplace dance on the walls and bed.

The peacefulness of the scene made the war and Libbor's army just outside the walls seem very far away. Ashes threw a fresh log on the fire. Sparks drifted into the room as the flames greedily lapped at the new log. Ashes found a chair by the fire and started to pull off his wet boots when he heard the city's warning bells. Cursing, he grabbed a pair of dry boots by the fire and pulled them on.

"What's going on?" Summer sat up in the bed and flung the blankets off of her. "Are we under attack?" Ashes was heading out of the door. "Sounds like Libbor thinks that he has waited long enough," he told her. "Don't worry, we can handle it, you stay here." the last was said as he run out the door

Even halfway down the hallway, Ashes had no trouble hearing Summer's reply. "Stay here?! Like hell I will!!"

China was standing in his paddock when Ashes ran in not bothering with a saddle he opened the gates, and swung up onto the stallion's back giving the stud a slap on the hindquarters. "Haaw! Go boy! Move! Get going!" China leaped forward forcing Ashes to grab a handful of mane leaning low against the horse's body he gripped hard with his legs. By the time that they reached the street, China was at a full gallop.

Ashes could hear the sounds of boulders from Libbor's catapults scoring hits on the city walls as China raced down the city streets. "They must have moved them closer." He thought. "Damn I should have known!" He had not thought that Libbor would risk losing any more of his catapults.

As Ashes rode up he saw the light of torches shined on the swords and armor of the men who lined the top of the wall. The Zlaroran catapults were flinging huge boulders onto the enemy's advancing army as fast as they could be loaded. Jumping off the stallion he ran for the nearest stairs and raced to the top of the wall.

China watched as his rider ran off. Then moved to stand under a tree close to the wall watching. Being a veteran of many battles and wars he knew he was not needed just yet, when his rider needed him he would come for him and the stallion would be ready.

Archers lined the wall loosing arrows from behind the ramparts at the line of men charging the walls. The archers shot as fast as they could draw their bows. Other men stood waiting ready to defend the wall from any of the enemy who got past the archers.

Spotting Nottie and Abby giving instructions to a group of men before they headed off down the wall he headed their way, Abby greeted him with a nod. "Libbor did not waste any time once we put out the gate fires. He either thinks that they did more damage than they did, or he is testing our defenses."

Nottie was watching the advancing men "I am betting on the last part. He has to know that fires did not burn long enough to do any real damage to the gate."

"Perhaps," Ashes agreed. "There is no knowing what is going through Libbor's head right now." He paused staring hard at the advancing line of men in the darkness.

"I see ladders but no ram. They are not going for the gate. They're going to try to scale the walls."

Shouts from down the wall told them that some of the enemy had made it past the archers and were scaling the walls already, drawing his sword Ashes headed down the wall to help repel the attackers. Ashes hurried, as fast as possible down the crowded walkway on the wall. By the time that he got there scattered fighting was breaking out where Libbor's men had succeeded in reaching the top.

An arrow shattered on the bricks of the wall behind Ashes making him duck his head. Before he could recover he felt someone grabbed his arm and he found himself being pulled over the wall by two men who were still clinging to their ladders. Bracing himself against the wall Ashes lunged at the closest man with his sword making the man release his hold on Ashes' arm.

Bracing himself against the wall again for leverage, Ashes pushed backward with his feet pulling the second man onto the wall with him. A sword came down on the man's neck, blinding Ashes with a spray of blood. The headless body toppled back over the wall and fell to the ground, outside of the city.

"Here, use this." a familiar voice said. Someone handed Ashes a rag that was torn

from the tunic of an unlucky man who tried to climb the wall. Ashes wiped the blood out of his eyes to see Summer, standing next to him. Her sword was bloody. "Stay here?!" she snorted, "and who would keep you alive if I had husband?" Not waiting for an answer she ran back into the fray.
By sunrise, the battle was over. Libbor's men had retreated. Leaving the snow at the bottom of the wall stained red and littered with bodies.

The assaults, on the walls came both day and night. For days at a time the catapults would pound both the walls and the gates. A boulder or burning barrel would sometimes make it over the wall, but never far enough to reach any of outer buildings or homes.

In the weeks that followed, the attacks came more and more often and each time it was becoming harder and harder to drive the attackers back. And as more and more of the enemy made it to the top of the wall, the fighting on the walls became more intense.

By the third month of the siege, they had managed to cut Libbor's numbers by half, but a fourth of Zlarora's army had been lost in the fighting. Of those who remained, over two hundred were too badly wounded to continue the fight. The rest were pushed to their limits, sleeping in short sprints and eating in fast gulps.

There had been no word from the men that Summer had sent to look for the Cocoans. Ashes knew that the men would not give up. He was sure they were either still looking or had died in the search. He would not believe otherwise.

To make matters worse, even without the fires, the catapults had managed to weaken the gates, the damage that the fires had done turned out to be worse than thought. In part, by same waters that had saved them, even as it put out the fires the water weakened the great hinges that held then in place. The fires had heated them red-hot. When the freezing waters had cooled them it had also weakened them.

With every hit, the gates were buckling, more and more. There was little that could be done. Ashes had as many men as could be spared reinforcing the gates, but even so, the gates would only last so long.

Summer slept fitfully, tossing and turning in their bed. Ashes watched her from the chair he sat in on the far side of the bedchamber. It had been three days since he had slept, and he had only eaten twice in that time. Despite Summer's urging. Even if he wanted to he could not sleep.

As quietly as possible, not to disturb Summer, Ashes went to the chest next to their bed and unlocked it taking out his saddle bags and sat them next to the chair by the fire. Opening them he took out the jewel that he had found in what seemed like a lifetime ago.

"Why?" he thought. "Why are you doing this? What have I done wrong? Please help me stop this war. "The light from the fire lit up the gem like a small sun but nothing else. Suddenly angry Ashes crossed the room and opened the patio doors a freezing wind blew the curtains back into the room as he made his way through the snow to the patio ledge.

"Damn you! Damn the day that I first laid eyes on you!" Drawing back his arm, Ashes threw the jewel high over the snow covered trees below. He watched as it fell into the small fast-moving river that ran through the garden and into the sinkhole to the underground river far below.

Suddenly, very tired, he walked back to the bed chambers, and to the warmth of the fire. He looked first to make sure he had not disturbed Summer then went back to the chair next to the fire slumping into the chair, he watched the flames. "How could I have been such a fool?"

A hand gently touched his shoulder. "Ashes?" Ashes looked up, Summer stood next to him with both love and worry in her eyes. "You need to sleep husband, it has been over three days. You cannot go on like this Please sleep, to make me feel better, if for nothing else."

Ashes' throat tightened, "Forgive me Summer. Please forgive me, I thought I was doing the right thing I tried to stop the wars. I thought that I could keep everyone safe. That I was doing the right thing." Ashes looked back into the fire." I was such a fool!"

Putting her hands under her husband's arms Summer lifted, trying to get him to his feet. "The only thing that you are being a fool about is not getting any sleep. You are no good to me -- or anyone else like this." She tugged on her much-heavier husband trying to get him up, "Come on. You need sleep, now! You are not thinking right."

"Summer, please, please, listen! I know I sound crazy I know I do, but hear me out please!"

Summer crossed her arms, "What is it that you want to tell me? Out with it! Then you are going to get some sleep if I have to hit you over the head with your own shield!"

"Summer," Ashes muttered, "If I were not a king if I could not give you all this, if I was nothing but a poor wanderer, a mercenary, would you have still have been happy? Would you still have married me? Loved me? Like you do now?"

Anger flashed in Summer's eyes. "What kind of foolish question is that?! Do you think that I only love you for your wealth?

Do you really think that I married you for your crown?" Stepping around in front of him Summer put a hand under his chin tilting his head Ashes looked up into her eyes. Summer's heart stopped at the look in his eyes. "Oh husband" she thought "what has happened, what is hurting you so?"

Summer's anger faded, the look in his eyes filled her with a deep dread. In all their years together she had never seen him like this, with such a look of fear and self-loathing in his eyes.

"You deserved so much more." Ashes muttered. "I could not give it to you. These people this kingdom, do not deserve what I have brought on them! I thought that I was doing the right thing! I thought that I could bring peace! An end to the deaths!" Summer had to step back quickly as Ashes suddenly rose out of his chair and crossed the room to point out the patio window. "Look! Look at what I have done to this city! To our people! To you! I am no king! No leader! I am nothing but a fool!"

Reaching out quickly, Summer grabbed Ashes' arm and pulled him around to face her. "This war is not your doing Ashes and the people know that! You did everything you could to prevent it and when that failed you did what any good man would do, you fought for the people and for the land that you love. That is what makes you a great king and a great leader!"

"Do you really think that these people love you because of your crown? That your men follow you into battle because of your crown? If you do, then you insult them Ashes. And if you think that I love you because of your crown, then you insult me."

Summer walked over to the bed, next to it two finely woven crowns sat in their holders on a large stand. Reaching down, Summer picked up the larger of the two and held it out as she turned back to face the man that she loved.

"Look husband. Tell me what do you see?" Ashes glanced down at the crown but did not answer. "You know what I see?" Summer went on, "I see an empty ring of gold, and jewels -- nothing more." Crossing over to him, she placed it on his head "You know what I see now? I see a great man, a great king, and a great leader."

Reaching up again, Summer lifted the crown back off his head and looked down at it. "Whether it is sitting on your head or not, it is still just a ring of gold -- and jewels nothing more."

With a backward glance Summer tossed the crown on the bed. "But with or without it. You. Are. A. King! It is what is in your heart, Ashes your soul, that makes you a king, not a crown."

Ashes stared hard into her eyes. "There is so much you don't know about me Summer I was such a fool -- not here -- but before. I thought that I could change things; make them better for everyone. I failed." Ashes voice dropped to a whisper. "I did not want to leave you Summer, I love you so much, but there was nothing that I could offer you but sorrow and pain. So I left. I'm sorry Summer. I am so sorry!"

A cold fear filled Summer. "What don't I know?! What are you talking about Ashes?! You're making no sense."

A deep ringing echoed through the city streets before Ashes could answer. "The gates!" Turning on his heels he ran out the door. Summer ran out the door behind him.

"Ashes wait, damn you come back! What are you saying? tell me!!"

Ashes glanced back, but kept on running down the hall. The look in his eyes hit Summer like ice water, "No!" she spat. "I am not losing you husband!" Spinning around she ran back into the room.

Moving quickly, she stripped off her night clothes and started to pull on her clothes and armor. Her hands and fingers felt like they did not belong to her moving slowly and clumsily. As she buckled the last strap she heard a horse racing down the street below, looking out the patio door she saw Ashes charging China down the street toward the gates. Watching him a cold hand clutched her heart, as she realized that he had been trying to tell her she would not see him again, and somehow that this was not the first time.

Ashes guided China past crowds of people running down the streets, many older women with children were heading away from the walls trying to get to the safety of the castle. Others were running toward the gates carrying whatever they could find to fight with willing to die if necessary, to save the city and those they love.

When Ashes reached the courtyard the outer buildings were already on fire and the courtyard itself was a mass of swirling men and horses. The gates were filled with masses of men streaming into the city. He spotted Abby riding Brian in the center of the fighting, swinging her swords non-stop as she faced-off against a much bigger man.

Vale and Calaco were at the base of the gates; the stallion was striking and kicking at anyone who came close. Vale used his sword to put a quick end to any of their enemies that the stud missed. Even Clip and Topper were in the midst of the battle the stump of his leg tied to the saddle as he used both his swords like a sickle mowing down any of the enemy who got too close.

Three men had Fredrex boxed in, the big man bleeding badly from a gash in his shoulder. Ashes charged China at the men shoving his sword deep into the closest one's chest, Fredrex used a backhand swing to knock another under China's hooves China struck out with a forefoot hitting the man in the back of the head. Fredrex finished the third man off. "Are you going to be ok?" Ashes ask Fredrex grunted in answer lunging back into the battle.

Ashes started to turn China back into the main battle when the stallion jerked then fell hard onto his side. Ashes jumped out of the saddle as his horse fell. He landed on his feet and spun around to see what was wrong with the stallion.

The breath went out of his body like he had been struck when he turned around. China lay on his side a pool of blood rapidly spreading out from his body. A spear-shaft was buried, deep in the stallion's chest. Libbor stood, just the other side of him, with a sneer of contempt on his face.

"I have taken everything from You Ashes, your army, your city, your people, your horse and after you are dead I will take your Queen!"

Ashes snarl and the savagery of his attack took Libbor by surprise. No one who knew him would have recognized him. Ashes had fought in countless battles in his life, but the one thing he had never done was to let his anger control his actions. This day, that changed. Here in front of him was the one man besides himself, that had caused all the deaths. Here was someone that he could kill with no regret.

Libbor's sneer quickly faded as Ashes pressed his attack, not letting up he drove the bigger man back. With every blow Libbor's swings were becoming more and more desperate. As Ashes pressed his attack, Libbor swung his sword, in a two-handed swing trying to use his greater weight to regain the advantage, throwing him off balance. Ashes ducked the wild swing, then gripping his sword with both hands shoved it hard into Libbor's chest.

Libbor's eyes widened with surprise and shock as his body sagged against Ashes' sword. Jerking his sword backward Ashes let the body fall, even before Libbor's body hit the ground he was running back to China kneeling next to him, Ashes lifted his head as the stallion took a last labored breath.

"Oh China, forgive me, friend!" Ignoring the battle, Ashes stroked China's soft muzzle. Something besides the horse's body flashed in the light of the burning buildings all around them.

The jewel! Staring in disbelief, he reached out and picked it up.

"How?!" Ashes muttered. "Why are you here? Why now? Is this what you wanted?!" Ashes' voice rose to a yell. "You promised me all that I could dream of; all that I could ask for, you lied!! I wish I had never found you, I wish I had never made that damn wish, I wish that in the desert I had just died! Please, if a life is the price for making a wish, take mine, don't make any more suffer because of my mistake."

Ashes knew from the sounds of the battle, that his last wish was wasted. Pushing himself to his feet, he started to rejoin the battle. When something hard and heavy hit him spinning him backward, Ashes looked down in surprise at the crossbow bolt sticking out of his chest.

His legs no longer wanted to hold him up. As he fell across China's body, "Forgive me God" he whispered, "All I wanted was peace, I did not mean for it to be this way." the sights and sounds of the battle faded as Ashes felt himself drifting, he felt strange. Not the fear and uncertainty he thought he would feel.

When his sight came back his was still drifting through what seemed like an endless fog. And there was something else, a sound, straining his ears he tried to make it out, someone was calling to him, the voice when he first heard it seemed very far away very faint, with each word it grew closer till he could hear each word as if the speaker was standing next to him.

"Fear not and mourn not, brother, and know that no lives were truly lost this day." Turning his head Ashes tried to find the speaker." Who are you, where are you? Show yourself!" Again, the voice spoke, seeming to drift closer, then further away.

"Well you know me brother, both now and in the desert, many times in the past months you have spoken to me."

Ashes voice was barely a whisper, "You're the jewel?"

The mist swirled, "That is part of what I am, yes."

Ashes voice rose, "Then tell me what has happened, you said that there were no lives lost, that is not true, I saw my friends die, my city burn, China, the most loyal horse I have ever known is dead! Are you saying their lives meant nothing?!"

Ashes felt a warm breeze calming him

"Peace brother, I will tell you what I am saying, you made a wish in the desert, you wished for peace, peace cannot be brought by one man alone, true peace can only come when all wish it, you had to see that for yourself."

"So it was a dream then?" Ashes asked. "None of it was real?"

His thoughts on one person in Particular "Summer!" the thought of losing her again hurt.

"There are many realities, this is just but one. Our actions today shape our reality of tomorrow. Reality is never set in one place. What you think of as a dream here, in another place, is a reality. What you think is real, is but another's dream." The voice drifted through the mist, never in one place, Ashes had stopped trying to find its owner.

"I want answers!" Ashes snapped "Not riddles! Was what I just went through a dream? That is all that I want to know. Did I just get a kingdom, and everyone, that I ever cared about killed because of my foolishness?"

"Foolishness?!" The voice seemed much closer now. "Look, brother, look and see the answers to your questions for yourself." The mist swirled again in front of Ashes, as a swirling mix of light and color that seemed to pull him into the center.

Ashes stood in the city courtyard once more. Remains of shops and homes were all that stood to tell that there had ever been a battle at all. The courtyard was busy with soldiers and citizens clearing the debris away.

Ashes looked around in amazement. "The city and the people are alright? But we were overrun, outnumbered, the city was burning, what happened?"

"You happened," came the soft whisper. "A king who was so willing to protect his people, that he stood in front of his men in every battle, who was never willing to let even the poorest of his people go hungry or cold, who cared for every life in his kingdom from the greatest of his generals to the cat who hunts mice in the barn as equal to his own, who gave a wandering people land and a home, where they could grow and prosper, who never saw himself as better than any of his people."

"When that king fell in battle, there was no army, no force great enough, to hold back the anger of his people, The cry and rally went from one end of the city to the next, Even the weakest, found the strength to strike back at their king's killers. Libbor's armies were driven back into the fields outside of the city. Just as the Cocoans arrived. You gave them a home and a second chance. They are a proud, honorable people. They came in answer to your call. Libbor's troops fled. The war is over!"

"You sought peace, Ashes, it was a good kind wish sadly you did not understand that even peace has a price no mortal man alone can bring peace, Many have tried, but for everyone who has tried there are hundreds who see such things as weakness they do not know or care about the suffering that their actions bring."

Ashes watched as Summer, his queen, walked down the main city street with Fredrex by her side. "Is she going to be alright?"

The mist started to swirl again. "Yes, she will mourn her husband's death as the city will mourn the loss of its king, but they will recover, death and loss no matter how hard, is but part of life."

"And now?" Ashes asked. "What happens to me now? Am I dead?" The mist swirled ever faster. "No, your life continues. Your fate is your own. There are many roads ahead of you, brother, which ones that you chose is your own decision. You must decide yourself, what it is that you want"

Ashes looked sadly at the swirling mist. "What I want most, I have lost for the second time."

"What was lost can be regained." The voice said knowingly. Again the mist stopped spinning and Ashes saw a familiar figure standing in a field, hoeing at rows of corn.

"Summer?" Ashes asked, longingly.

"She has not forgotten you or stopped loving you." The voice went on. "Many men have courted her, and she has forsaken them all. She waits for one man, you and you alone can decide if she has waited in vain."

"All of this time and she still loves me -- after what I did to her?!" Ashes' throat tightened. "Where is she? Is it far?"

The voice grew faint again as the mist started spinning around Ashes till he felt that he was being pulled into a whirlpool "Follow the sun three days ride from where you awaken, at the foot of the tallest pike you will find her. Farewell, my brother, and take heart when you awaken, for in the eyes of your brothers, you will always be a king!"

Ashes woke with a start as something pushed against his chest. He opened his eyes to see a long face with large brown eyes staring at him. Ashes leaped to his feet. "China!" He yelled, throwing his arms around the horse's neck joyfully. Ashes hugged the horse, running his hands through the stallion's mane, "I thought that I lost you. I thought that I would never see you again!"

The stud lifted his head, snorting, as his rider let go of his neck. The oasis and the pool were gone, all that remained was a single tree. With his saddle bags and water jugs filled to their limit.

Ashes saddled and bridled China, then tied down the saddlebags and the water jugs. He swung up into the saddle pausing to look over his shoulder at where the pool had been.

"Whether a dream or real, I still am not sure." Ashes said. "But I promise you this, I will never again raise my sword in battle unless it is to protect myself or those that I love, if ever there is a time when all men work for peace, I will stand beside them."

China pulled impatiently at the bit and Ashes let the stud have his head trotting over the dunes.

Ashes did not see behind him, as the dust of their passing settled...Sands under the single tree began shifting on their own in ever-growing waves. Growing slowly at first, then ever faster grass began growing here and there. Trees burst out of the ground spreading green leaves out to the sun. A small trickle of water started to seep out of the ground flowing faster and faster till the ground in the middle of the new oasis was filled with a bubbling pool of water. The sun shone on the water, lighting up the stone pedestal, in the center, were a sparkling jewel sat waiting....

For In the distance, over the dunes, a rider comes.

About the Author

Vaughn Hansen is the middle child of seven children, two sisters and four brothers. He was born in Ontario, Oregon and grew up in Tooele, Utah. As a young man he worked as a ranch hand, helping to break wild mustangs and working with cattle and sheep in Nevada, Wyoming, Oregon, and Montana. He spent four years in the army before moving to Indiana with his sister Amy who shares his love of animals, to start a small farm where they take in older and disabled animals.

www.ingramcontent.com/pod-product-compliance
Lightning Source LLC
Chambersburg PA
CBHW051217160726
47994CB00002B/635